THE GATEWAY

Jon Hart / Joe Black

www.icebergauthors.com

Jonathan Hart

This first book of many is dedicated to my mother Moretta Hart. Until we meet again.

Joe Black

This is dedicated to my Hood. R.I.P. Pooky Head, Baby Huey, Buttah Man, OG Chris, OG Rob. Shout out Fleetwood, hold your head.

Chapter 1

HER CAPTOR WAS NOW IN FULL VIEW. He stood about 6'2" and looked like he weighed a solid 200lbs., all muscle. Those dreamy ocean blue eyes a girl could only fantasize about had turned into an all-out storm. Vanessa could see her body in the mirror of his eyes. It was as if his eyes were playing out the scene before it happened. Vanessa's body had become some unfortunate ship that had just met head on with Hurricane Rita. The angry blue water tossed her from side to side, at times slamming her against the windows of his lenses. Water filled Vanessa's entire body but she couldn't drown in his eyes, instead the water was ripping Vanessa apart from the inside out.

His blonde hair was now covered with some sort of stocking cap and his hands bore medical gloves. How could someone so angelic in looks be so devilish in deeds Vanessa thought? The last thing Vanessa remembered was following him up his stairs and him letting her into the house. He had stabbed Vanessa with some type of syringe releasing something into her blood stream that had rendered her unconscious. Vanessa had awoken tied up, naked, and terrified. Vanessa wondered if he had raped her. Vanessa didn't feel like she'd been penetrated, and now she didn't know if that was a good thing or a bad thing. Bound by zip ties on her legs and feet, Vanessa was at the mercy of this monster.

"Are you comfortable Vanessa?" he finally spoke.

What kind of question is that? I'm tied up for Christ sake! How could I possibly be comfortable? Vanessa thought.

"Yes I am" she responded, "but I think I might be more comfortable if you were next to me."

He stared at her in silence, surprised by her response, but not the least bit fooled or deterred from his plans for Vanessa. "Well, let me help you feel uncomfortable," he suggested as he walked over to her.

"No, please don't" sobbed Vanessa uncontrollably. Her words were muffled and mutilated by tears and unquenchable fear. Her hysteria heightened as he drew closer. "Nooo," she screamed as he closed in. "Mi---" but before her words could form he stabbed her in the floating rib with an ice pick, connecting with all bone. The pain was explosive, her breath became short and dizziness soon began to encompass her. He grabbed Vanessa by her jaw bone and squeezed it as tight as possible.

"How comfortable do you feel now?" whispered her assailant ever so softly into her ear.

Vanessa couldn't believe what was happening to her, but it was. This was no dream, and it sure as hell wasn't a movie. He left the ice pick inside Vanessa and stepped away. Vanessa's whimpering had turned into a mountain of tears and uncontrollable shakes. All Vanessa could do was watch as he gracefully walked over to a wall and turned off the lights to the cellar. Darkness engulfed the room. Vanessa cried louder, pleading for help. Unaware that her prison was soundproof, Vanessa continued to scream, but to no avail. The house Vanessa was destined to die in was so dead that it couldn't even feel the vibration of her words.

Unknown to Vanessa, with each scream her captor grew closer. Vanessa screamed so loud flashes of white light rapidly streaked through her mind. The intensity of despair had overwhelmed Vanessa causing her to lose all sense of reality. As she hollered and whimpered he quietly removed a pair of black leather gloves from his back pocket and slipped them on. He readied his mind, blocking out all of Vanessa's screams. The blow caught Vanessa off guard practically knocking her out, but what came next made her wish it had. He followed with a combination of knees and elbows curling Vanessa into the fetal position. He repeatedly kicked her in the face and stomach; grunting and making unintelligible noises as he allowed the pleasure of losing self-control fuel him.

Finally, out of breath and curious to see the damage he'd done, he strolled over to the light switch and turned it on. Vanessa being unrecognizable was an understatement. Her face was plastered with hair and blood, purple engulfed her body, making her look like an anorexic Barney that just fought Mike Tyson in his prime. Vanessa's breaths were short, it was as if a hole was somewhere in her lungs causing air to escape as she struggled to inhale and exhale. All Vanessa could do in her broken shattered state was wonder what in God's name could she have done in this life or any other life for that matter to deserve something like this.

Leaving the lights on her captor exited the cellar and went into the kitchen. He fixed a peanut butter and jelly sandwich, added a little honey in the middle and poured a glass of milk. This was his favorite snack, been that way since he was a kid. After he finished eating he locked up the house and went out to the garage. He got into his car, and paused for a moment before starting his cruise home. The maniac took slow deep breaths, inhaling deeply through his nose and exhaling slowly through his mouth. He relished in the high of destructive dominance for a while before heading home. All the maniac could think about during the ride home was Vanessa. Her porcelain skin had looked like a beautiful vase that had just shattered into shards of glass. Deeply focused on his upcoming task the Maniac had lost track of time and realized he was now behind schedule. No worries he thought to himself, as he turned on his cruiser lights, and sped all the way home. No worries at all.

Chapter 2

Mr. Maniac lived in Brookline Massachusetts, a quiet, safe neighborhood. A police officer living on the street never hurt the crime stats either. He moved swiftly through his home, everything was already prepped and ready to go for the final stages of the masterpiece he'd been working on. He jumped in the shower and let the hot water consume his body. No matter how hot he made the water, nothing could dent that cold nothingness that whirled in his inner core.

"Rough day at work Michael" asked his wife as he slipped into bed?

"Not really, the usual drug dealers and crack heads."

She pulled him closer, he loved the way he felt and looked in her arms. Her ebony skin was dark chocolate, giving life to his pale dead arms. Their children laid sleep in their own room, ages three and six. Those two boys were the most important people in Michael's world besides his wife Candice. The most important people in Michael's life and they were all under one roof. Tonight was going to be the hardest part of Michael's life and mission. He was thirty-one years old, married for seven years, an officer for ten, and a psychopath his entire life.

For the past two years Michael's murders had been focused on fellow cops and their families, with a few indiscretions like Vanessa here and there. The body count was seven officers, ten children, and fives wives total. After all the murders, Michael burned the houses down with gasoline along with the victim's corpse's still inside. To ensure a good burn Michael always doused the bodies with gasoline, he also ran an IV of gasoline through the bodies to maximize the burn potential. Michael would extract the teeth of all his victims prior to setting the fire. He would then leave one tooth from each victim in a gift wrapped box. For no other reason than profiling kicks, Michael would tie a green and red bow around the box on the front lawn. It was funny watching F.B.I specialist trying to figure out or piece in the meaning of the green and red bow. There was the Christmas theory, the birthday gift theory, even a dirty cop blood money theory. The F.B.I came up with all types of stupid shit. It wasn't until Detective Ramsey took the case that the fun got spoiled. Ramsey quickly dismissed the ribbons as a red herring and soon after the ribbons stopped.

Tonight would be Michael's family's turn. Michael had come to terms with his role in life, he was more than just the grim reaper. He wasn't merely an angel of death; Michael was the gateway to hell. His family and job were holding him back, but to just leave wouldn't be good enough, to be death one must be dead to the world as the world knows it. Michael already had his tooth and his kid's teeth from past tooth fairy deposits.

"Are you okay baby? You seem distracted," questioned Candice as she stroked Michael's face in a way only a loving wife knows how. Without a word Michael slid out of bed and walked into the bathroom. Candice watched as her husband walked into the bathroom. When Michael returned he was holding a gun with something that made the barrel look longer.

"Michael, what's going on baby? Talk to me, what's wrong?" Candice was lost, and had no idea why her beloved husband was now pointing a gun at her.

Without a single word Michael pumped two rounds into Candice's gut. Michaels's wife of seven years was about to experience a slow agonizing death. Usually Michael savored in the moment of his craft, but not tonight, tonight's murders were necessary, simply business. Michael would take no pleasure in the events of tonight.

The walk down the hall to his boy's room felt like what he imagined the walk down the corridor in the movie Greenmile felt like. All Michael could hear is Percy's voice, but instead of Percy announcing loudly "dead man walking" he was declaring "death is coming." Michael stared at his oldest son Michael Jr., lying fast asleep in his superman pajamas. His brother Seth lay in the opposite bed wearing Sponge Bob pajamas. Michael found himself tearing up. These were his boys, he taught them how to fish, play baseball, football, and how to defend themselves. Michael read to them, took them to work sometimes to show them what he does in the office. Michael would do anything for his boys, his edge and will to go through with the task at hand was fading.

It's not your fault Mikey. This doesn't mean you hate them, in fact it means you love them more. You can't take them on our journey, and besides they'd only get hurt along the way. This is best for all of us kido, so like Candice just do it and be done with it.

The Voice was gone. Michael never spoke to the Voice, only listened. He'd tried as a kid to talk to the Voice, but the Voice never answered him. The Voice never steered Michael wrong though, even in his tightest moments, when it seemed like Michael would be caught for sure, the Voice always seemed to bring him out.

Michael walked over to each of his sons and administered a general anesthesia. Michael placed the bodies in the living room and laid them all on the floor. Candice had passed out from the loss of blood, and her pulse was extremely weak. After giving Candice a local anesthetic to the mouth Michael quickly set up the gasoline IV's for his wife and children. Next he began to remove the teeth from everyone. The amount of anesthesia Michael used for his boys was enough to keep them asleep for the procedure. Four bodies lay on the floor, all prepped and ready to burn. The fourth corpse was a male, fitting Michael in height and weight. Michael had found him stumbling downtown one night, and had kept the vagrant alive in his lair long enough to pump him with an IV full of gasoline.

Michael could barely stomach pulling his wife and kids teeth out. He found himself continuously tearing up during the process. Michael collapsed in despair as he looked at his own hands covered in his wife's blood. Michael took a moment to gather his bearings and then placed Candice's tooth inside a box, alongside his boy's teeth and one of his. Once he was done with pulling teeth and setting the IV's Michael doused the bodies along with the entire home with gasoline. Michael slowly walked to the doorway and struck a match. And with a flick of the wrist and toss of a match Michael said goodbye to his life as a police officer, a husband, and a father.

Chapter 3

Detective Ramsey arrived at the scene around five AM, with the fire still ablaze. Ramsey had been on call 24 hours a day since the fifth cop-family murder. Tonight would make it the eighth cop family murder. Ramsey knew Officer Sloan, he thought of him as a good cop. Sloan never had a complaint filed against him, he brought in good collars, and he never had a problem with the blue wall of silence. Ramsey was determined to catch this monster at any and all cost. Since being assigned to the case Ramsey had lost his wife and kids through divorce. Ramsey's wife couldn't take the lonely nights anymore and started having an affair with her high school sweetheart. Shortly after the affair started she filed for divorce and custody of the children. Ramsey didn't fight her, and all he asked was that she didn't keep him from seeing his boys, which she agreed to do. Ramsey had lost a good cop and an even better friend behind this cop killing freak, and that in turn sparked a determination in Ramsey to bring this storm of death to an end.

Ramsey watched as firefighters fought to put out the blaze. A uniformed officer hustled over to Ramsey with a small box in his hand.

"Found it on the lawn sir, I didn't open it, but I guess you already know what's inside" stated the officer.

Ramsey nodded his head slowly, acknowledging that he did know the contents of the box. Ramsey took the box from the officer. The box felt like the officer had just dropped a hundred-pound dumbbell into

Ramsey's hand. Ramsey didn't even bother to open the box; instead, he began to walk his to his car.

"Sir, where are you going?" asked the officer.

"To the lab. Once the fire's out, tighten the sealed off area and don't let anyone cross that line other than the fire department investigators."

"When will you be back sir?"

"As soon as BFD clears the scene for us to get in there" answered Ramsey as he walked away.

Ramsey didn't want to be at the scene, he knew it was a waste of time. Ramsey had no choice though, protocol would require him to investigate the scene once the fire was out and the fire department concluded their investigation. Ramsey took this time to kill two birds with one stone: Ramsey needed to get away from the scene, and the contents of the box had to be run over to the crime lab. Ramsey knew how many teeth would be in the box and who they belonged to. Ramsey was not only familiar with Officer Sloan, he was aware of Sloan's wife Candice and their two boys.

Ramsey was a Boston homicide detective. Although the murder had taken place in Brookline, Ramsey had jurisdiction over any and all cases linked or believed to be linked to the serial killer. The newspaper had dubbed the killer "Inferno", but Ramsey didn't think it was cute at all. Being a cop you make enemies everyday so someone trying to kill a cop wasn't hard to imagine. But it wasn't just cops being killed; women and children were being brutally murdered for no other reasons than that they were the wife and the kids of police officers. Ramsey felt like he was dealing with more than just a serial killer, he was hunting a terrorist.

Chapter 4

The forensics lab was located on the outskirts of town. The lab served as a morgue as well, making things a lot easier for purposes of the case. The lab was primarily used for federal cases, but Ramsey had access to anything his heart desired concerning the cop killings. Ramsey made it to the lab in record time.

Ramsey walked into the basement morgue. With all the time Ramsey was spending here with the forensic specialist Kinkay, the morgue was something like a second home.

"Hey Dr. Kinkay" announced Ramsey with enthusiasm as he walked into the lab.

Upon entering the lab Ramsey immediately noticed a hamburger sprawled out on the table with fries peppering the surrounding area, a coke dripped sweat as it waited for Kinkay's death grip to clench and slurp its life away. Ramsey used to wonder how Kinkay worked so efficiently around such an environment, and how for Christ sake could she eat with that smell of death in the air?

"Well hello to you to Mr. Sunshine" smiled Kinkay.

Ramsey had been spending a great deal of time in the forensic lab since he was assigned to the Inferno case. Ramsey was still shocked by how uncomfortable the cold air made him feel. Kinkay had a habit of working with her lab coat unbuttoned, because she was well endowed, it made it hard for Ramsey to keep his eyes on her face. Dr. Kinkay had long black hair and stood at 5'8". Kinkay's skin was an odd glowing sun kissed color that reminded Ramsey of October leaves in New Hampshire. Kinkay was wearing her hair in a bun, held in place with a few properly placed bobby pins. In spite of Kinkay's poor eating habits, Ramsey never could figure out how she managed to stay in such great shape. The woman had the body of a Nubian goddess but she ate like a velociraptor. Watching Kinkay eat had to be by far the hardest thing for Ramsey to see, it was comparable to a crime scene. Yellow empty cheeseburger wrappers littered Kinkay's desk. Ramsey observed french-fry crumbs at the heel of a fresh corpse laying on the table. Kinkay's lab decorum only mirrored her eating manner, in all his years of service Ramsey had never seen a more chaotic forensic lab then the one Kinkay operated. The oddity of the situation is that Kinkay is the most intelligent, creative and efficient forensic tech Ramsey had ever encountered. Ramsey tossed the box onto Kinkay's table amongst the empty soda bottles and mini snicker wrappers warring for rule of the territory housing blood samples and other sensitive forensic material.

"Damn girl, you really are the master of organized confusion" stated Ramsey as he flicked away a snicker wrapper. "Anyway, I need this done like yesterday" finished Ramsey.

"Another one huh? This is crazy, we have to get this dirt bag."

Ramsey observed Kinkay as she made preparations to examine the contents of the box. Kinkay didn't have what you would call conventional beauty but Ramsey couldn't help his overwhelming attraction for her. Ramsey wanted to take Kinkay right then and there on the table. Her intensity for the job made her magnetic. The job was like a drug for both Ramsey and Kinkay, and they were just two junkies basking in heroin heaven.

Kinkay was from Saudi Arabia; Ramsey had personally recruited her a few years back when he was in Afghanistan on a covert operation of the highest national security level. It was Kinkay's expertise in dental forensics that made her such a valuable asset in this particular case, but had Ramsey remembered what it was like watching Kinkay eat he might have reconsidered.

"Yeah another one, but I got a good feeling about this one" lied Ramsey "Now I need you to keep your eyes peeled for the slightest detail."

Kinkay looked at Ramsey and her lip slightly twitched, he had spent enough time with her to know that meant she was getting nervous. Ramsey had that effect on women in general. Women loved Ramsey for all his natural qualities: good looks, extremely high IQ, athletic ability, but most important his loyalty and honesty. Ramsey always seemed to know what to say when it came to the ladies.

Ramsey and Kinkay's bond was different than what he shared with other women. Back in Afghanistan while undercover Ramsey had saved Kinkay's life. With all the education and degrees Kinkay had obtained throughout her life, she was still just a slave to an abusive husband. Fortunately for some and unfortunately for others, the abusive husband was Ramsey's target. At first Kinkay was just a means to get close to her husband, but things turned for the worse and Kinkay's life had fallen into danger. Ramsey jeopardized the entire mission to save Kinkay. Shunned in her country and with no financial means to survive, Kinkay accepted Ramsey's job offer to work in the United States.

Ramsey couldn't take the smell of food and death for too long so he left the lab quicker than he planned to. Ramsey was wound up with no way to release it. A few years ago he would've smoked a whole pack of Molboros by now. Quitting that monster was one of Ramsey's greatest accomplishments. Ramsey pulled out his phone and made a call.

"You awake?" asked Ramsey dryly. The person on the other line yawned out a slow yes. "Don't sound like you are."

"I'm always awake for you sugah, how long will it take for you to get here?"

"Ten minutes and put it on my tab."

"That tab is getting pretty long baby. We'll be at twelve after today."

"I know. I've been putting in a bunch of overtime this week. I'll take care of you."

"Well alright darling, you just shimmy on over here, and I'll be waiting for you."

The line went dead; Ramsey closed his phone and started his car. He didn't bother checking his emails, texts messages, or voicemails. All Ramsey wanted right now was to get a load off. Cherry's southern accent melted Ramsey from the first night he met her hooking downtown while he was off duty. His immediate intention was to bring her into the station for a scare, but on the ride Cherry's voice had enchanted Ramsey and instead of the police station, Ramsey and Cherry ended up back at Cherry's apartment. Cherry stood at a solid 6 feet, she was four feet of waist, legs and ass. Cherry was more of a mahogany brown, with deep big brown eyes. Her hair wasn't that long but she could wear a weave with the best of them. Her build was more athletic than anything else and Ramsey chalked that up to Cherry's basketball career. During her freshman year in high school Cherry lead her school to its first women's basketball championship. Sadly, during that same year Cherry's dad was killed by a stray bullet during a police shootout. The loss of Cherry's dad hit Cherry's mom so hard that she lost her job and started using drugs. Things got so bad they had to move back down south from there New York home in Brooklyn. Cherry's mom didn't change and her family quickly washed their hands of her. Help was extended to Cherry but she didn't want to abandon her mother, so Cherry stayed by her mom's side. The constant moving and living in filth made life literally unbearable for Cherry. School and basketball had soon become a distant memory; pain and suffering were the only memories that seemed to resonate anymore. The way Cherry fell into prostitution reminded Ramsey of his mother and her career as a prostitute. Oddly enough Cherry reminded Ramsey of himself, and all those years he spent as a child protecting his mother, or least feeling like he had to. Ramsey was smart enough to know his relationship with Cherry was unhealthy, and that in some twisted way his dealings with her correlated with his childhood. Their relationship was a perfect example of Socrates's Oedipus theory

Since Ramsey and Cherry's first encounter, Ramsey had spent enough money to put Cherry in a house with no mortgage and a paid off Lexus. Of course no regular cop salary could afford to do that, but Ramsey was no regular cop. Ramsey worked both sides of the shield, along with a few colleagues he'd grown up with. Ramsey's right hand man and fellow officer was a lead detective for the drug unit. Whenever a bust or investigation involving large sums of cash or drugs presented itself, Ramsey would take the intelligence and weigh all the options. Ramsey's final decision to hi-jack a stash was based heavily on risk factors. Ramsey's counterparts felt Ramsey was too cautious at times, but in the end they always trusted his final decision. Ramsey's small knit crew had a whole community to push the drugs and cash through, making life just a little easier on the financial side.

Ramsey didn't care about circumventing the law for personal gain, his outlook on drugs and crime was one of simplicity. People liked doing drugs, and nothing was going to change that, and where there is a demand there's a market. America not only created a market for drugs, it continuously builds around the infrastructure of the drug trade: employing law enforcement, the judicial system, drug treatment programs, all creating opportunities for the private sector to build and own prisons, detention centers, halfway houses and other government funded institutions. Ironically enough investors in these ventures were mainly made up of buyers that were predominantly made up of lawyers, judges, politicians, and other people closely related to the laws which incarcerate the people in which they benefit off of.

The only thing that bothered Ramsey was senseless violence. People killed over money, that made sense to Ramsey, but to kill for the mere thrill or pleasure, or because someone looked at you wrong or stepped on your sneaker, made no sense to Ramsey at all… Which is was another reason why Ramsey was taking the serial killer case so seriously.

Chapter 5

Michael drove in silence. He usually played a little Elton John, Michael Jackson, The Beetles, even some hip hop every now and then, but at the moment, Michael wasn't feeling up to anything.

Mikey, it had to be done. Look I know you loved them, but they would never understand our purpose in life. Imagine the hurt you would feel if she ran out on you and took the boys. Or how about if you got caught the news would destroy the image your wife and children had for you. This works out for all of us, now we can focus on our true task in life, we're the Gateway, and without us, no man shall enter. Hey I know what'll cheer you up. Let's go say hi to Vanessa.

Michael like the thought of that, he quickly made his way back to his lair, but he still couldn't help wondering what life would be like from here on. In a sense Michael thought his responsibilities as a father and a husband kept his chaotic side in check, giving him a sense of morals and values. Now he had nothing and no one, except the Voice Michael thought.

And I'm all you need Mikey.

Michael hated the fact that the Voice could hear his thoughts, but he'd learned to live with it. Once he arrived at his lair, Michael put on his stocking cap and gloves before entering the house, made a stop in the kitchen and then made his way down to the cellar. Vanessa had balled herself into the corner; she'd been in that position for the past few hours. When she first noticed his presence Vanessa didn't have that usual look of fear in her eyes his victims normally possessed. Instead, she looked defeated and defiant all at once. Michael attempted to hand Vanessa a blanket, but she wouldn't reach out for it, he then approached her with caution. He placed the plate of food and blanket on the ground and moved in closer on Vanessa.

"I'm not going to hurt you ok? Ok?"

Vanessa just watched Michael as if she were a serpent waiting for the right moment to strike. Once close enough Michael pulled out his hunting knife, Vanessa never even flinched, Michael was impressed. He cut her zip ties, walked back to the plate and blanket and handed Vanessa a PB and J sandwich, no honey and a glass of milk.

"Eat, you'll need your energy" said Michael.

"Why are you doing this to me?" mumbled Vanessa through her swollen jaw and missing teeth.

"What was that dear?" questioned Michael as he knelt down next to Vanessa.

"I said why are you doing this to me? I thought you liked me."

"I do like you, which is why I'm going to usher you in, I'm going to be your ticket into paradise. Through my hands your soul will be sent into a world where no one can hurt you. But the only way to reach this paradise is through pain, the shedding of blood, and then death."

With that said Michael rose and walked over to a tall dresser that was more like a closet. Vanessa's fearless persona had vanished and she was once again sobbing uncontrollably. Besides the closet like dresser, the boiler was the only other thing in the cellar.

The dresser was huge with two doors taking up most of its height, with a chain and padlock linked between the two handles. The dresser was solid oak with black trimmings giving it a rustic antique look.

Michael fished his keys out of his pocket, undid the locks, and swung both doors wide open stepping to the side so Vanessa could take in the scenery. The sight of the contents within the cabinet doors caused Vanessa to almost faint. The dresser was filled with swords, spiked bats, spiked ball and chains, spears, hunting knives, and other objects Vanessa never got a chance to view.

Michael put on a pair of leather gloves over the medical gloves he was already wearing; he then reached in the dresser/cabinet and pulled out a top of the line nine iron and a special hunting knife he placed in his back pocket.

Wonderful choice Mikey.

With her last bit of strength Vanessa pulled herself up using the wall as a brace. She barely moved as she fought to drag herself alongside the wall.

Oh this is going to be fun (chuckling) ok now Mikey, remember, it's all in your form.

Michael wound up and swung as hard as he could, he made sure his form perfect, his extension superb. The club made a thick thud noise as it struck Vanessa square in the left ear.

Hole in one Mikey. I told you with enough practice you'd get it. And the crowd goes wild, Mikey, Mikey, Mikey, Mikey.

Vanessa slid to the ground. Michael never let go of the nine iron's handle as he dropped his arm at the same rate in which Vanessa slid to the floor. Vanessa was dead well before she ever made it to the ground. Michael watched as her blood flowed to the center of the cellar where a small drain sat. Michael smiled at his work, this was his tenth kill with the golf club and he finally got it right. On his past nine attempts the club landed on the cheek, different parts of the ear lobe, but never dead center inside of the ear. Michael had gotten so mad during the past failed nine attempts that he just wailed on the victims until they were a pile of putty.

Gutsy little thing she was, now let's see what they look like.

Michael pulled out his knife and knelt down next to Vanessa, he then rolled her over so she lied face up. Michael tilted Vanessa's head back, arching her throat forward. He plunged the knife deep into her throat and began carving down. Whatever resistance he ran into by bone or tough flesh Michael merely put a little elbow grease into it.

Once he reached the uterus Michael flipped over the body and repeated the process. Once all the blood was drained from Vanessa's body Michael removed a tooth and then carefully wrapped it in a piece of plastic. Next Michael wrapped her body into a black tarp and carried Vanessa to the trunk of his car. Once the body was secured Michael walked back into the house and went upstairs to his den. Michael went to the drawer that he kept locked, pulled out his keys and opened it. Michael retrieved a passport, a social security card, a birth certificate and bank statements. The house he owned was under one of Michael's many aliases and the documents he took were of his new identity, James Patterson. Michael chuckled at the name, it was his favorite author. The Voice had Michael set up the identity along with many others years ago. The Voice also had Michael enroll in night school once he graduated from the police academy. With no specific major Michael took courses in psychology, biology, world history, American literature, micro and macro-economics, health, web designing, he even knew German, French, Spanish, Portuguese, Latin, Russian, Japanese, Chinese, Vietnamese, and over a hundred African dialects. Michael's wife had always wondered how he managed to get so much accomplished in such little time. To Michael being a cop and learning came easy but fulfilling a purpose made for you and only you, now that was hard.

Everything Michael did in the house he did with a stocking cap and gloves on, so removing any trace of him being in the home was easy. Michael had even shaved all the hair from his body except his head to reduce the possibilities of leaving hair samples. Other than the documents in the dresser the only other things in the home were peanut butter, jelly, honey, milk, and a little silverware. Just to be sure there was no evidence of his presence, Michael went over the house with a rag, and numerous bottles of bleach and ammonia. Michael was forced to take numerous breaks on the front porch because of the strong smell. Once Michael reached the basement he didn't use any of the chemicals or cleansing products on anything except the dresser and the boiler. Michael didn't allow any of the chemicals to touch any of his murderous tools either. Michael never cleaned his weapons of mass destruction, or the floor, which was now stained with thousands of blood passages all leading to the same drain and into the abyss. Once the house was sterilized Michael exited the home leaving the front door unlocked and a box on the lawn. On his drive to the airport Michael took out a cell phone and placed a call, he got the answering machine and left a message.

"Twenty-two Andrew Lane."

Chapter 6

Ramsey's phone rang but he ignored the call, he was busy deep inside Cherry. Ramsey knew her real name; in fact, he knew a lot more about Cherry than she cared for him or anyone else to know. Leaving Cherry with a state of mind that she was in control of the situation made it a little more exciting for Ramsey.

"You ok baby?" questioned Cherry after Ramsey rolled off of her.

"I'm fine, it's just this case has me all out of whack, another cop and his family are dead."

"People die every day sugah. It's not how you lose your life that's important, it's what you do with it while you have it that counts."

"Well I'm gonna use whatever life I have left to stop this guy. I'm sure glad my wife left me, who knows, I might've been on the list up until she divorced me."

"Now that's just plain old fools talk sugah."

Ramsey stood up and stretched while Cherry secretly admired his features. Ramsey was 5'5' and 165 pounds of all muscle. He was Asian and Black, with fine jet black hair, his mother was a prostitute so his father's identity was a mystery. It was only by Ramsey's features that he and his mother knew his dad must've been of Asian descent…… What part of Asia, only God knew that? Cherry cooed over Ramsey's small girl like feet, in her head she thought, so much for the big foot theory.

Cherry noticed that Ramsey's hair was longer than usual, Ramsey had told her he was going to get braids but she thought he was only joking. In Cherry's eyes Ramsey was the furthest thing you would expect from a cop, but maybe that's why he's so damn good at his job, he thought differently. With all of his degrees and all of his higher education Ramsey managed to think at a street level, giving him a slight advantage over most cops and criminals.

Cherry was secretly in love with Ramsey. Once she got her living situation under control the money he gave her for sex, she in turn used for her education. Cherry was two semesters away from a Bachelor's degree in criminal justice. With no kids and no job responsibilities other than sleeping with Ramsey Cherry was able to earn her associates degree within three semesters. Cherry was studying to be a criminal lawyer and she hoped once she graduated and started working that Ramsey would someday start dating her for real and later on propose to her. If all else failed, Cherry planned on proposing to Ramsey herself.

Since Ramsey had started dealing with Cherry she hadn't been sleeping with anyone else. She ran out on her pimp and used prostitution as a cover whenever she had class or needed to study late and couldn't entertain Ramsey. Ramsey knew all about Cherry's school life, and what she'd been doing, he was actually proud of how she made the best out of a messed up situation. But Ramsey's feelings for Cherry were only sexual.

"Your phone was ringing earlier," Cherry reminded him. Just as Ramsey was about to check his voicemail his phone rang.

"Ramsey."

"I got something for you" busted Kinkay through the phone. "The boy's teeth weren't pulled out, they fell out."

Ramsey paused to process the information.

"Did you hear me?"

"Loud and clear, I'll be there in twenty minutes." Ramsey hung up the phone and quickly got dressed.

"Must be some special lady to pull you away like this sugah" smiled Cherry on the outside with a scowl on the inside.

"She sure is Cherry; in fact, she's the greatest woman I've ever met."

Ramsey bolted out the room and towards the door. Once in his Lincoln Town car Ramsey threw on his sirens and sped all the way back over to the forensics lab, and this time he truly made it in record time.

Chapter 7

"Lay it on me babe" Ramsey huffed, still catching his breath from the non-stop run from the car, up eight flights of stairs, and down the hall.

"Well I just took the time to go over all the other teeth x-rays from the other crimes. Sloan's children were the only children whose teeth weren't pulled out. At a glance you may not notice but with a little observation you can see the decay that started setting on the teeth. One is a little more advanced than the other, but there close in time of falling out."

"Fell out?"

"That's what I said sunshine."

Ramsey sat down for a second to think about what this new development in the case meant. "What about Sloan and his wife?"

"Both teeth were pulled out like everyone else's."

"Why would the killer pull everybody's teeth out, children included and not Sloan's kids, it's not making any sense?"

"Maybe his conscious is finally getting to him, maybe he doesn't want to do it anymore."

Ramsey ignored Kinkay's theory. When it came to forensics Kinkay was unsurpassed, but when it came to thinking like a sociopath or any criminal for that matter Kinkay was a dodo bird, or was she? Suddenly pictures of family day and sporting events where cops brought their family reeled through Ramsey's mind. Sloan was a dad like none other, he loved his boys more than life itself. Sloan kept more pictures of his two boys on his desk than any other cop Ramsey had ever seen. Sloan talked about his boys like God had crafted them in front of him and then handed them to him. Ramsey tried to shake the idea from his head but he couldn't. Sloan was the killer, he had to be, and as heartless as it was to believe, Ramsey was convinced he was on the right path.

"It's Sloan" said Ramsey without looking up at Kinkay. "I can't prove it yet, but I think Sloan is the killer, and now he's a walking ghost."

"Ramsey that sounds a little far-fetched, besides why would Sloan use these teeth when he still pulled out the rest of their teeth? It just doesn't make any sense."

Ramsey pondered Kinkay's logic for a second. For a reasonable person this train of thought made perfect sense. Sloan could have just as well used one of the teeth he pulled from each of the boys like he did all the other children and this new development would not be under review. But a reasonable person wouldn't butcher countless families let alone his own. But how could Ramsey prove it? Sloan had been pronounced dead, and there was no hard evidence that gave any credence to his hypothesis. But Ramsey's gut feeling was telling him he was on the right path, and when you grew up in the streets like

Ramsey did that's all you had most times to go off of was a gut feeling. Ramsey's gut feelings had helped him survive growing up; it's what made him the most sought after cop in the country. Ramsey had received offers from the FBI and the CIA and had turned them both down. If there was one thing Ramsey hated about the system it was politics, besides Ramsey was already dirty, and the potential these positions brought for skimming off the top was more than he thought his circle could handle.

"I'm gonna check out of here Kinkay, I got a lot on my mind I need to clear out."

Kinkay was a little disappointed to see Ramsey go, but she'd worked with him long enough to know he worked best alone. "Okay Ram, I'll be available when you need me, call me, ok."

"Sure."

On the drive home Ramsey tried to rationalize in his head how Officer Sloan could possibly be Inferno. Ramsey only had two things to base his hunch on, but he'd solved cases with less. First, Ramsey always suspected that Inferno may be a cop. Despite the carnage Inferno left behind, the crime scenes were always as clean as a freshly picked nose. Second, the boy's teeth. The inconsistency was a red flag like no other

Ramsey was so deeply absorbed with trying to make a connection with the killer it was as if the killer had infiltrated his mind. Every turn and stop Ramsey made was operated by some sort of internal GPS.

Ramsey was right in his killer's shoes and about to look into his killer's eye's when his voicemail reminder went off. Ramsey checked the single voicemail he had, and without a second thought he threw on his lights, racing to the address conveyed over voicemail, Twenty-two Andrew lane.

Chapter 8

On his way to Logan Airport Michael had no idea where his life was headed, so he silently waited for The Voice to speak. He wondered why the Voice told him use the boy's teeth that naturally fell out and not the ones that he had pulled, why the hell was he still driving with a body in the trunk, and why on earth did he call Ramsey's phone and leave the address to his lair? Things were becoming complicated to Michael; he had no idea as to if he was going up or down. It was like he was falling down a hole and never reaching the bottom. Lost in thought he almost rear ended a Mercedes Benz, instinctively he started to slam on his brakes.

No, swerve right you idiot

Michael went to the right and missed rear ending the Benz along with getting rear ended himself by a Honda that was tailgating him way too close.

Ok it's obvious you need some answers so you can refocus. What we did was we left clues, for the great detective Ramsey. He's our, how do you say, Matlock. He's the Giuliani to our Gotti, the Captain America to our Red Skull; he's our Alex Cross in the flesh. I know you've been having doubts about our position in life, so I needed to show you that we're destined for this role. Without ever speaking on it, we both agree that Ramsey is the best cop we've ever met. He's been offered positions that only a mad man would turn down. If what we're doing is wrong we will be caught, and it looks like he's the only one that can do it. But everyone needs a little help, and that's what we gave him. From here on in we stick to the script. We left him enough hints to put him on the right trail. If he doesn't catch us then my point is proven, this is our destiny.

Or maybe he's just not the Alex Cross we've been waiting for thought Michael to himself. Once at the airport Michael parked the car in the lot and went to check in for his flight. He was headed to California; he had a date with a plastic surgeon. He hated what he was about to do to his face but The Voice said it was necessary, because he had a face that no one could forget. The Voice said he didn't want Michael to touch his beautiful face either, but with great purpose comes great sacrifice. Michael felt he'd already made the greatest sacrifice when he shot and barbequed his family.

Michael boarded his plane in complete silence, avoiding eye contact and any type of small talk, but once he was seated his plans were foiled. A slim black woman with braids sat next to him, her hair was like Queen Latifah's in the movie Set It Off. But she had no features like the Queen. She was a red bone with full lips and dimples, when Michael stood so she could take her window seat their eyes locked and you could cut the chemistry with a knife. He didn't get a good look at her body, but from the little he saw he knew that she was holding a nice ass. Her face was clear except for a few freckles around her nose that made her more Rudy Huckstable adorable than sexy, but he was still captured by her.

"Anybody ever tell you, you look like Brad Pitt?" grinned the red bone,

"I've heard it a few times, but I never see it when I look in the mirror"

"So what do you have planned in the sunshine state?" questioned the red bone.

"Just a little vacation from work, a little surfing, maybe tan a little, hit on some beach babes, you know, the usual"

"Sounds like fun, I'm taking a vacation myself. I'm in into real estate, but the market is so awful right now that I figured I'd get away for a little while, get my wind back and return with a vengeance."

"So where in Cali are you staying?" asked Michael

"At the Marriott in LA, and what about yourself?"

"I haven't decided yet until now, looks like it'll be the Marriott", grinned Michael.

I bet her pussy is virgin pink. Look at the size on that thang. She's got a camel foot.

"Now what makes you think I want you staying at the same hotel as me" flirted Redbone.

"What makes you think what you want matters" smirked Michael.

Now that's how you talk to these bitches Mikey.

"A man that goes for what he wants, I like that. Now what did you say you do again?"

"I never did, but since you insist on knowing, I'm a writer. No I haven't been published yet but I have three offers on the table. I'm playing the hold out game to see who breaks with the best offer. So for income I sell stock"

"What kind of novels do you write?"

The kind that tortures and kills dumb bitches like you.

"I write children's books, I'm working on sort of a Harry Potter type series at the moment, but the bulk of my work are short stories with an educational theme."

"Sounds cool, so what do you do in your spare time?"

Bitch if you only knew.

"I like to fish, cook, and go dancing, read, and exercise. But mainly I like to wrap myself around the lady of my life."

"Oh so you're seeing someone?"

"Not anymore, she moved on."

"Why'd she leave?"

"I guess our time was up, I still love her, we're still good friends, just minus the intimacy" smiled Michael. "So you have nothing to worry about."

"I encourage a little competition, it's good for the soul, nothing wrong with a little fight" grinned Redbone, allowing her dimples to sink in, making her that much more irresistible.

"I'm James by the way," said Michael as he extended his hand.

"Michelle. Pleasure to meet you James," grinned the Redbone as she shook his hand.

Oh yeah, well get ready for the fight of your life bitch.

Michael and Redbone talked the entire flight, which suited them both just fine. Taking the Red Eye can be boring if you have nothing to do, and for Michael boredom was the equivalent of death.

Chapter 9

Ramsey pulled up to Twenty-two Andrew lane. He didn't bother calling for back up or getting a warrant which was one of the perks of being a super cop. The first thing Ramsey noticed when he arrived on the scene was a large cardboard box in the middle of the front lawn tied with a perfect green and red bow. Ramsey immediately pulled out his weapon, observing each available window with a lock on his position. Ramsey had pulled his firearm many times in the line of duty, and had taken his fair share of human life. But in that single moment, standing there in the open like a wounded duck (another position he'd been in plenty of times with no worries) Ramsey felt helpless.

Ramsey walked past the box and headed straight for the front door. Before Ramsey slowly entered the home, keeping his gun raised close to his body. The house reeked so bad of ammonia and bleach Ramsey had to pull out a handkerchief and cover his nose and mouth. The front two rooms of the house were empty, no pictures, no furniture, nothing. Upon entering the kitchen Ramsey was a little disturbed. This had to be the cleanest kitchen he'd ever stood in. nothing was out of place, the toaster sat neatly next to the microwave. The table was nicely dressed and decorated with flowers. An old 1970's radio stood caddy corner to refrigerator. The fridge was all white without a hint of stain. Ramsey checked the cabinets; unopened jars of peanut butter ruled one cabinet, while jelly and honey ruled their own separate cabinets. The brands were all the same, Skippy peanut butter, Smuckers jelly, and Bumble Bee honey.

Ramsey checked the fridge next. Inside the fridge were a half jug of milk and a quarter of a jar of jelly. The freezer compartment contained nothing but frozen jugs of milk. Ramsey glanced back at the table, the half a peanut butter jar and the bottle of honey with only a squeeze left sent firing pins off in Ramsey's head. He had racked his brains trying to put a face with the voice on his answering machine but nothing had registered. Ramsey quickly made his way out of the kitchen and up the stairs. Sweat beaded onto his brow as he engaged every unknown corner of the house. His left index finger melted into the curved groove of his six shot revolver, dubbed The Governor by the firearm circle. The Governor is a snub-nosed double action Smith and Wesson revolver built on the Z-frame with a lightweight alloy frame weighing a mere 30 ounces. It can fire 2½ inch .410 shotgun shells, .45 Colt, and .45 ACP. Ramsey had the Governor's trigger pull altered to 3 pounds of pressure from the standard four. For that reason, The Governor was illegal in Massachusetts. Every room upstairs was bear with white walls, all except one. Ramsey entered a room with blue wallpaper decorated with trains. A bunk bed rested in the corner next to a lamp stand. Both beds on the bunk bed were turned down, the idea of the killer being two people had never crossed Ramsey's mind, but the bunk had to have some sort of significance. Ramsey checked the drawer to the lamp stand, it was locked. The closet was empty and there was no other furniture to check. Ramsey made a mental note about the stand and proceeded back downstairs.

Ramsey made his way to the cellar. For some reason the darkness of the cellar, mixed with the eerie dissension down the stairs didn't move Ramsey. In fact, he felt more at peace with the unknown environment he was entering. It was as if the darkness generated a raw energy that Ramsey could feel tingling all over his body, his "spidey senses" were going crazy. Ramsey never pulled out a flash light, he was one with the darkness, and he could glide through her void as if gravity no longer existed. Once at the bottom of stairs Ramsey took a full two minutes two observe the room. He made out the dresser to far corner, along with a light switch off to his right, the boiler was off to his left, and besides that, nothing appeared to be in the cellar. Ramsey turned on the light; suddenly the darkness was being chased away as light flooded the cellar. The light captured the cellar so quickly Ramsey had to cover his eyes to adjust. The first thing Ramsey noticed with the light was the fresh blood that mingled on the cellar floor with dried up blood. All the blood flowed towards a drain that lied in the center of the cellar.

Ramsey made his way to the cabinet like dresser. The doors on the cabinet were wide open as if the contents were on display. Upon observing the cache of weapons, Ramsey couldn't help but notice how blood stained each instrument of death. The neat arrangement of the weapons caused the dried blood on them to form a rhythmic flow that gave its own detailed story on how they came to be. Ramsey surveyed the cellar one last time and then made his way towards the exit.

Ramsey had a nerve wracking feeling as we walked onto the porch and pulled out his cellphone. It wasn't the cellar, or the blood, or the various weapons the unnerved him, it was the countless stories that cellar told that made his heart beat faster.

"Captain, it's Ramsey, I need our entire forensic team and a bomb squad unit out here to Twenty -two Andrew lane, post haste."

"The entire team, are you fucking stupid Ramsey, I've got a triple homicide on top of the cop killings this morning, I can't do it."

"I think I've found the cop killer's lair, and I think it's more than just cop killings he's been committing."

"How'd you find that, and why wasn't I informed?" yelled the Captain.

"The killer left a message on my cellphone with just an address; I wanted to check it out before I called anything in."

"And what makes you think it's our guy?"

"A huge red and green bow, and blood Captain, lots of blood."

Chapter 10

"Oh James, oh James," moaned the Redbone as Michael thrust himself in and out of her from behind. He grabbed her by the tails of her braids and slapped her on the ass, keeping everything in a perfect motion.

"I'm cumming, I'm cumming, oh my God you feel so good."

Okay Mikey, let's make this nut count.

Michael moved his left hand across Redbone's face, resting his palm on the lower right side of her chin. Michael was a little nervous; he'd never tried this maneuver before.

Don't worry Mikey; just make sure you use all your strength and do it quick. Trust me, this is going to be classic.

Michael could feel Redbone's body tense as she began to moan deeper from her on coming orgasm. Michael raised his mount on her to get a better angle and grip. With his left hand positioned at the base of her chin Michael quickly placed his right hand at the base of the back of her head and with all his might quickly spun Redbone's head to the left. The snap was quick, the break sounded like a twig that you snap in half unexpectedly. Redbone's body went limp as Michael exploded inside of her. It was the most wonderful feeling Michael had ever had. He rolled Redbone's body over so she was facing him, the look of surprise and pleasure that encased her face caused Michael to smile. It was art in its purest of forms and Michael was the artist.

Now if you gotta go, that's the way to go, right Mikey? Now let's get the hell out of here.

Michael took his time getting dressed, he could still smell Redbone's sex scent in the air, and it was invigorating. Michael used all the alcohol from the mini bar along with a bottle of rubbing alcohol he'd found in the bathroom. Michael walked over to Redbone's body, he was captured by her beauty. She reminded him of Candice a little bit, they favored each other in the eyes. The thought of Candice sent Michael into a controlled rage. Without feeling Michael rammed the bottle of rubbing alcohol into Redbone's vagina and emptied its contents inside of her. After soaking Redbone as good as he could with the alcohol from the mini bar, Michael dismantled the fire alarm and sprinkler system in the room, and set the place on fire.

Michael thought about his surgery that was scheduled for tomorrow as he exited the hotel, he figured he should enjoy his face one last time. Michael stepped into a cab that was conveniently parked in front of the hotel for guest.

"Where you headed buddy?" cheesed the Arabic cab driver in a high pitched tone with a very deep accent.

"It's a new day my man, take me to the coast. I wanna see ass and titties and foam flowing from beer mugs," smiled Michael

"I know just the place, so buckle up. This is gonna be a ride"

Michael was in a world of his own now, everything was surreal. All Michael could see as he gazed out the window were beautiful colors, colors that he could manipulate into the most glorious of paintings. Michael was an artist, who felt like the world was his canvas.

Chapter 11

"All I want inside is our forensic team, everyone else secure the perimeter, and start going door to door asking neighbors about the person or people who live here" announced Ramsey to about 20 cops and forensic specialists standing in front of Twenty-two Andrew lane.

"This is crucial evidence, and the last thing I need is some idiot fucking up my crime scene" finished Ramsey.

Captain Furnari had finally arrived in his all black Lincoln town car, fully suited in his uniform. The press had arrived shortly after Furnari did; Ramsey knew Furnari had called them. Ramsey didn't have the clout to pull every forensic agent in the office and field to one scene, calling Furnari was a necessary evil. Ramsey didn't mind the press; this just wasn't the time to have them involved. The last thing Ramsey wanted was information being leaked to the press, or worse, an overheard misunderstood conversation. Luckily Ramsey made it his personal business to know all the forensic agents in and out of his district personally, so his trust and confidence in the men and women at his crime scene were pretty high.

"Why are all these cops out here? Let's get inside and find out what we can so we can stop this shithead" yelled Captain Furnari. Furnari was short with salt and pepper hair. His Italian ancestry gave him a rich olive colored skin tone. At 5'6' Furnari was the most hated captain throughout the state as well as the most powerful. In Ramsey's eyes Furnari possessed what is called a "little man's complex." Furnari belittled people whenever he could; to Ramsey it was just the complex kicking in whenever Furnari did that.

Furnari had gained his position through his wife's family. Marrying the Governor's daughter was the first major move made in Furnari's plan to obtain wealth and power. Furnari was the most incompetent Captain to ever grace the title, with no field experience whatsoever on his jacket, Furnari was a joke behind closed doors. For all those reasons Ramsey started and maintained his career under the employment of Furnari's district. Ramsey was Gapeto and Furnari was his Pinocchio, but lately Pinocchio had been acting like a real brat.

"Sorry captain, this crime scene is too sensitive to let any of the boys play. I need perfection on this one, as we should have at every crime scene."

Furnari gave Ramsey a glare that could've cut a slice out of the air. Furnari was no fool; he knew Ramsey had used his ignorance to the position as a means for Ramsey to get what Ramsey wanted. But what could Furnari do, Ramsey was not only his best cop, Ramsey played mind chess better than anyone he knew. Ramsey never took credit for any of his big arrest; he always awarded his great police work to the tutelage and guidance of Furnari. The flip side of it which burned Furnari was that behind the wall of the shield everyone knew Ramsey never even consulted Furnari during investigations.

"Okay team" started Ramsey as he addressed the forensic team. "I want Kinkay and her team in the cellar, Peter; I want your people in the kitchen. Sanders, your team is going to commandeer the rest of the home. I want every inch of this house dusted for prints, if there's a piece hair anywhere in this house I want it found. After you've checked it once, check it again, and when your eyes cross from focusing so long I want you to check it again. We are not going to find a print, or hair in any of the conventional places, although we're going to check them all. The print or hair that we find that is going to crack this case wide open is going to be an accident made by the killer. It's up to you to find that mistake, that lack of judgment, or absent minded slip up that can bring this killer right into the crosshairs of the Governor."

Ramsey pulled Kinkay to the side as the teams made their way into the house.

"The cellar and the kitchen are our most important areas. My guess is the other team won't find as much as a piece of lint. I'm just praying we get lucky, I need you to be on your 'A' game down there Kinkay."

"What's down there Ramsey?"

"Long hours, and years of paperwork."

Once the forensic teams were inside Ramsey walked over to Furnari and asked to speak in private. Ramsey wanted to pursue his hunch on Officer Sloan, but he knew investigating a cop was considered bad business. Ramsey wanted as little exposure on his investigation as possible, however he knew he would need permission from the higher ups to conduct the investigation legally.

"What is it Ramsey?" asked Furnari dryly.

"I want to run a silent investigation into Officer Sloan. I have reason to believe he may be the Inferno."

"Reason to believe?" questioned Furnari. "I haven't seen any evidence come across my desk that would suggest this."

"That's because there is no evidence sir. I have a hunch, which is why I wanna pursue it quietly."

"Let me get this straight, based on no real evidence you want me to allow you to launch an investigation against a decorated officer, right after his murder. Are you outta your fucking mind Detective?" Furnari's accent had become very thick.

"Sir I just want a little rope with this one."

"No fucking way, and if you already started, shut it down! The last thing I need at the heart of this fucking psychopath killer is a gotdamn badge. Now you listen Detective, and you would do well to heed what I'm telling you. This conversation never happened."

"Sir, one way or another, I'm takin this bitch down. I won't let innocent people continue to be hurt."

"Fair enough. And if our friend does turn out to be a cop, I never wanna hear about it detective. Not me, not anyone. Are we clear Detective?"

Ramsey looked over Furnari's shoulder to see his best friend and fellow officer, Deebs walking up. Deebs pulled up a little while after the forensic teams had all gone into the house.

"So whadda we got here bro?" asked Deebs.

"Looks like the killer's lair. He called me with the address."

The look Deebs gave Ramsey could only be responded to with a shoulder shrug and the biggest "I don't fucking know either" look you could imagine.

"Anyway, I need to know if we on for tonight" asked Deebs

"El Hefe give the okay?" questioned Ramsey

"Yeah yo. I got the heads up that the money might get moved tonight, so we gotta be ready if it do."

"I don't know about this one Deebs, we need more information."

"I hear what you sayin bro, but Tommy and Dread are ready to move my nig. We already passed up on one opportunity to move on that bread. I don't know how many more chances we gon get at this kind a stick."

"So what do you think?" asked Ramsey

"You know me man, I move if you say so homey."

"I'll call when I'm done here and I'll meet you at the spot in a little while."

"Aight, don't be too long, cuz if I get the call it's gonna be soon."

"I got it D, don't worry."

Ramsey got lost in thought for a second as he watched Deebs walk away. Deebs was Ramsey's best friend, along with Tommy and Dread. The four of them had been friends since they were kids. Deebs worked in narcotics while Tommy and Dread worked in S.W.A.T. unit together. The four of them had grown up together in Boston on a small side street. Had it not been for Lt. Martin they would have more than likely ended up being your average street thugs, with the exception of Ramsey of course. Ramsey was a leader and a go getter in any situation he was in, even if no one else knew it. Lt. Martin was a dirty cop that worked out of the Mattapan B-3 precinct. Along with being the five dirtiest cops in Massachusetts they were also the most known and respected officers throughout the city of Boston.

The four had started out as kids running with a street gang called Monster Squad. The Monster Squad gang was also known as the Murder Unit or MU for short. Deebs was the oldest of the four with Ramsey only a year younger than him. Tommy and Dread were the same age, but technically speaking Tommy was the baby of the four. Lt. Martin had heard about the four boys but it wasn't for anything serious. That was until the four of them had become suspects in a multiple homicide. For reasons unknown to the four at the time, Lt. Martin had taken a particular interest in the four. Lt. Martin had made arrangements with all four of the boy's parents to give them a chance to make something out of their lives before they ended up dead or in prison for the rest of their lives. In light of the boy's living situation it wasn't hard to get the parents to agree. Deebs and Tommy were brothers whose parents were at war with a heroin addiction. The streets swallowed them with ease. Ramsey was an only child in a single parent home, his mom was a recovering prostitute that loved her son with all her heart but was too damaged to grasp the concept of parenthood. Dread was the only one of the four that Lt. Martin had a little trouble getting the parents to agree. Dread was raised in a God fearing home. His parents did their absolute best to raise a respectable boy with a bright future. With three older sisters Dread was just what his name said, a dread to anyone he had no emotional attachment to. But for his own good Dread's parents let him go with Lt. Martin and low and behold the four of them ended up with a success story.

Chapter 12

Matt and Marr watched as Michael entered the bar. They were both taken by his uncanny resemblance to Brad Pitt. Matt whistled a melody insinuating his interest in Michael, Marr replied with a whistle agreeing. Both men were blonde haired and stood over six feet. They each contained a slim muscular athletic build. Marr had a smooth oily face with a skinny short pointy nose. Matt contained almost identical features with exception of a nose peppered with freckles.

Michael spotted a gorgeous petite older redhead nursing a bloody Mary in the corner of the bar alone. Michael wasn't much into cougars but there was something about the woman, and it didn't hurt that she was absolutely stunning.

She looks like a winner Mikey.

Michael casually walked over to the redhead, "mind if I wash away some sins with you?" smiled Michael as he pulled up a seat.

The redhead turned to Michael with a look of surprise. Most men were more intimidated by her looks than intrigued. Redhead positioned her body to face Michael. Something is different about this one said the Redhead to herself. Michael reeked of confidence and something else, something that drove Redhead wild on the inside.

"Sure, so what's your name handsome?"

"James. So what's a pretty girl like yourself doing in a place like this?"

"Same thing a handsome guy like you is" grinned back Redhead.

"Oh and what's that" chuckled Michael as he scooted closer to Redhead.

Redhead leaned close to Michael's ear, her lips slightly brushed his ear lobe as she slowly whispered, "HUNTING."

Ok Mikey, time to go something's off here my dude.

Michael immediately stood up to leave only to have Redhead grab him by the wrist.

"Where're you going darling? The party's just getting started. Sit back down and let's have that drink you were talking about."

Mikey, let's fucking go, this bitch is trouble.

As much as Michael wanted to leave, something about Redhead had smitten him severely. Physically white women never did anything for Michael, but there was something about this one that had captivated him. It didn't hurt that she had the perfect hour glass shaped body with a pair of titts that sat up like a dog expecting a treat. Her red lip stick was slutty and classy at the same time. How'd she pull that one off thought Michael? Redhead chuckled.

"What's so funny" asked Michael with that confused smile look you get when you don't know if someone is laughing at you or with you.

"Nothing" replied Redhead smoothly.

Matt whistled to Marr.

"Looks like we have a love connection."

"So it would appear" whistled Marr.

"Do we dare break up whom God has united?"

"I suppose it would be improper to interfere with divine work, but then again I do believe we fell in love with him first."

"Will the two of you fucking faggots quit that goddamn whistling" yelled a local patron of the bar. Although Marr was the eldest of the two he was definitely the immature one as well. And that didn't mix well with his short temper. Sensing the blood rushing to his counterpart's head Matt quickly belted out a little Beethoven, one of Marr's more favorite calming melodies. Marr responded with the theme song from the first "Kill Bill" movie.

"I think we found our replacement my good man" answered Matt.

"Correction my dear friend, he found us. Shall we go prepare a welcoming?"

"It would be quite rude if we didn't wouldn't you say?"

Matt and Marr paid their tab and exited the bar whistling different tunes.

"That was weird" said Redhead as she watched Matt and Marr exit the bar.

"I can't say. I was busy staring at you" replied Michael. "What's your name?"

"Heaven"

That's it Mikey, time to get the fuck up, let's go.

"You look nervous" lightly laughed Redhead "how cute, don't worry James, I won't bite. So whaddaya say James, I'm parked right out front."

Michael was so spellbound by Redhead all he could do was nod yes. Redhead took Michael by the wrist and led him out of the bar and out to the parking lot. Michael noticed the two guys that were staring at him when he first entered the bar, standing across the street leaned up against a blue minivan, smoking cigarettes.

Matt and Marr started whistling the theme song to "Love Boat" as they watched Redhead and Michael make their way to a bloody red B.M.W. Matt and Marr watched as the lights blinked on the car and Michael slid into the passenger seat while Redhead got behind the wheel.

"Nice car" said Michael as he melted into in the plush leather seats.

Okay Mikey last warning bro, get the fuck out of the car, we need to go now.

Why so paranoid Voice? Mikey's gonna be ok. I'm Seduce. Voice, that's an odd name, not very creative. More cliché if you ask me. Heaven, say hi to Voice.

"Hello Voice" said Heaven while staring at Michael.

Michael had been staring out the window when Heaven said hello. Michael whipped his neck around fast enough to snap it. The look on his face was indescribable in every sense of the word.

"Don't be frightened Mikey" said Heaven as she reached out for Michael's hand. "They're talking now."

Chapter 13

Matt and Marr watched as the drunken patron that verbally assaulted them stumble into his car. The man was about 6'7' and built like an ox with a pot belly. The drunk donned a short army haircut, with a beat up fatigue jacket. Matt whistled a question to his partner...

"Do we follow?"

"Are you jesting with me my young chap? Of course we follow"

Matt and Marr jumped into their all black death van and followed the blue beat up dodge that their drunken mark drove off in. They whistled the DMX song "Where the hood at" as they followed the car. They didn't bother trying to be inconspicuous about it; they stayed right on the tail of their prey.

"What the fuck is that damn van following me or what" said the drunk out loud. He reached under his seat and pulled out his forty-five. "Well if these muthafuckas wanna play, I'm all game". He placed his gun out the window and let off four shots. Matt let out a long whistle.

"It appears our friend is armed."

Marr paid the gunfire no mind, in fact he sped up and hopped right on the tail of the Dodge. Marr mashed the gas and slammed into the back of the 1981 burgundy red Dodge Diplomat, causing the car to fishtail off the road. The drunk struck his head on the windshield and dropped his gun. Before the drunk knew what was happening Marr was on the driver's side. He punched through the already cracked window and grabbed the man by his collar. Matt calmly whistled the theme song to Kill Bill while he watched his partner work. The drunk had regained his senses and began to put up a fight. The drunk managed to break free from Marr's grip and scrambled for his gun which had fallen on the floor of the passenger side. Marr pulled a stun gun from his pocket and placed it in the small of the man's back sending enough volts of electricity through his body to paralyze the man instantly. Marr dragged the man back out of the car, but stumbled at the weight of him. Matt strolled over to help and whistled, "Looks like you need to hit the gym my good boy."

"I think you're right ole boy, now let's make haste and get out of here."

They dragged the body to their van and threw him in the back. Matt got into the driver seat while Marr dealt with the drunk. Marr strapped the man to a gurney tying his arms and legs to the side hand rails of the gurney leaving the rest of his body exposed. After securing the man Marr got into the man's car and followed Matt. Matt drove whistling Lyfe Jennings "Must be Nice" to himself. In about twenty minutes he pulled into their garage, located in the back of the home. Marr quickly parked the man's car next to the van and made his way to the van. Marr flamboyantly pulled open the doors of the van. Never abandoning his theatrics Marr gracefully boarded the truck and unlocked the wheels on the gurney. The man was awake now, his eyes were frantic and bug eyed as he screamed. The man was trying his best to still appear menacing from his vulnerable position. Marr grinned sinisterly as he pushed the gurney out of the van. The gurney crashed to the floor, flipping on its side, by now the drunk was awake and mumbling something neither of them could make out. The garage was connected to what the two referred to as the surgery room. The room was decorated with every kind of weapon you could think of, from mid evil times to the latest Sci-Fi weaponry. Marr whistled to his partner

"Do you mind if I work alone my good friend?'

"I'd be honored to watch a master such as yourself work, proceed my dear lad." Matt walked over to the camera system they had set up in the room and flipped the record switch on. Marr waited until the drunk was fully aware of his surroundings.

"What the fuck are you doing? Let me out of here you son of a bitch."

Marr smiled at the man and slowly sliced his shirt open with a scalpel.

"So this how it ends for a war hero huh? Two fucking fags cut me open on a..." but before he could finish his statement Marr grabbed him under his jaw causing his mouth to fly open. With the speed of a mongoose he took his other hand and reached into the man's mouth and pulled his tongue out as far as he could. Then with one swift motion he released the man's throat, swept up his scalpel and with one stroke cut the man's tongue completely off. Blood gushed everywhere as the man screamed in pain, but it was more than pain that caused the man to scream so loud. It was pure horror; he finally realized he was in the presence of Satan's Spawn.

Matt whistled "such a crude and vicious thing the tongue can be."

"You're so right my friend; I believe the bible speaks on how the tongue is as a double edged sword"

"And clearly this man needed to be disarmed, so vile and obscene. "I think this is the first time we've performed a civic duty for the community"

Marr smiled as his partner began to whistle the theme song from Kill Bill. Marr moved like Dr. Ben Carson as he sliced the man's chest to the rhythm of the tune, each slice going deeper and deeper until the man's chest was covered in blood. The man didn't know what to do, tears rolled down his eyes as blood flowed from his chest. He started to become light headed and was fading in and out of consciousness. Marr made sure every cut was precise, staying away from major arteries and major intestines. He stepped back to admire his work and slightly tilting his head to the side. He then walked over to a jar; the man was barely conscious and couldn't make out what was in the jar. Marr opened the jar and dumped close to fifty leaches onto the man's chest and stomach. His work was complete. Matt and Marr walked out and left the leaches to do their work, they would watch the video later over breakfast in the morning. They walked silently side by side through the corridors and entered into an elevator. The elevator music played a piece from Bach as they rode up. The elevators stopped and they stepped out into a luxurious living room, red satin decorated the entire room. Original Michelangelo's, Picasso's, and Nichii paintings adorned the walls. The fire place burned pieces of oak that elevated a sensual smell throughout the room. The Grand Piano played Mozart while the theatre sized television silently played live news coverage from Iraq. Matt spoke to Marr.

"Care for something to eat"

"No, I'd rather not wake Elizabeth, besides it's too late to put something on the old tummy."

"True indeed, true indeed."

With that said the two M&M killers retired to their own rooms for the night.

Chapter 14

The bomb squad pulled up to the scene in full force about fifteen minutes after Furnari had arrived.

"Damn Calhoun what the fuck took you so long?" barked Ramsey in a joking manner.

"Don't start with me Ram" growled back Calhoun. "I've been running around all fucking month 'cause of these gotdamn bomb threats. a person even thinks bomb and we're getting called."

Ramsey liked Calhoun for one reason and one reason only; Calhoun always spoke what he felt.

"And why the fuck do you need the bomb squad anyway, your guy is hands on from what I know."

"Momma always said, 'better safe than sorry boy,' plus I knew Furnari would put a pep in his step once he heard the words killer and bomb. He's ready to do some ungodly things to beat the feds to a potential terror strike."

"Fucking Furnari, you know that fucking prick winked at my wife at the last family and friend picnic?"

Everyone had heard about the infamous wink, and Calhoun had refused to let it go. Had it not been for Ramsey's mediator skills it would have turned into an all-out brawl.

"Man just clear the fucking box so I can check it out and you can get the fuck out of here."

Calhoun stormed off to work on the box with the rest of his team. Ramsey took a few moments to contemplate the recent developments within the past twenty-four hours. He knew the killer was evolving, but it was happening unexpectedly. Nothing seemed to be a mistake with this guy, everything he did was deliberate, which frightened Ramsey even more. Ramsey knew the cop killings would stop and that if he didn't catch the killer soon he probably never would. Ramsey pondered on what could be in the box. Holding true to form the box should have one tooth from each member of some family that the killer had butchered. But the box on the lawn was the size of a mini refrigerator. Ramsey couldn't figure out what was in the box, was it just one tooth, the tooth that held the key to piece the whole puzzle together? Or was it a bunch of teeth, and if so would it be teeth from previous victims or unknown victims? Why did the killer give up his lair thought Ramsey, where was the killer at now, and was he butchering a victim as they spoke?

"Is that fucking box cleared," screamed Ramsey out loud to no one in particular. Ramsey's head hurt, there were too many questions circling in his head and not enough answers.

"All clear detective dip shit" yelled back Calhoun as he and his men loaded up their SUV and swerved off.

Ramsey hop skipped right to the box which was already open. His eyes nearly popped out of their sockets as he looked at the mountain of polished teeth that sparkled inside of the box. Some of the teeth had a hint of grey to them while others were shining yellow from decay. But it was the mountain of shiny white teeth that really turned Ramsey's stomach. Ramsey could tell from the different stages of decay along with the number of teeth that the body count just touched heaven. Ramsey just hoped that the teeth weren't just one tooth from each victim.

Ramsey pulled out his cell phone and called Kinkay for an update.

"We've gotten blood samples from everywhere" replied Kinkay. "From the floor, the walls, the weapons, the dresser, the boiler, the stairs, even the ceiling."

"Any prints anywhere?" questioned Ramsey. He figured there wouldn't be, but he asked anyway.

"Actually that's what I'm dealing with now, there are hundreds of prints everywhere."

Hundreds thought Ramsey, and none of them would be prints from any of the victims from the cop killings. None of the victims had been dismembered and nothing suggested that the victims were killed hours before the fire. Ramsey didn't know what to make of this, it was like the killer was exposing himself. And there it was, it hit Ramsey like a ton of bricks. The killer was finally saying hello, introducing himself to Ramsey and the rest of the world.

"Okay Kinkay here's what I need you to do. Get every print you can, I got a box full of teeth I need you to check out as well. Then I need you to do a missing persons check for the past three years. Pull all the dental records that are available for the missing persons and cross reference them with the DNA samples for matches. Then get in contact with any friends or family members connected to the missing persons and see if they……."

Kinkay cut Ramsey off "uuhh excuse me Ramsey, I work in forensics, and tracking down people sounds more like detective work."

"Sorry" replied Ramsey. "I just got carried away, finish up what you're doing and let me know when you're done."

"God, lighten up Ramsey. I was just busting your balls, and you know I wanna catch this fucker as much as you do. I'll do anything you need me to."

"No, you're right. Forensics is your specialty and I need you to be on top of your game. Thanks anyway though." Ramsey broke the connection before Kinkay could retort. He knew his feelings would never get in the way of his job, but he worried about Kinkay. But now wasn't the time to worry, Ramsey needed information and some time to think.

Ramsey was on a tight schedule and he needed to deal with the situation with Deebs and the rest of the guys. Ramsey's current dilemma was that the case had just did a 180 and he didn't want to leave his crime scene under Furnari's supervision. Just when Ramsey was pulling to his wits end detective Berta Jenkins pulled up. My angel in a uniform thought Ramsey to himself. At thirty-nine Ramsey had a little less than a decade on the force. Ramsey's rise to homicide detective was faster than your average rise. Ramsey had cracked two very high profile cases by running counter secret investigations in his early years as an officer. Mixed with his military background and Captain Martin's ability to pull strings the transition to homicide detective was fairly easy. Berta Jenkins was an up and coming homicide detective. Berta Jenkins was a young intelligent black female raised right in the heart of Dorchester. In Ramsey's opinion, she was the best thing to happen to the force. Her heart was comprised of all the good things it took to be a good cop. She was loyal, concerned about the community, smart, and brave.

Berta Jenkin's chocolate complexion stood at 4'9' with a double D breast size. Watching Berta run use to be the funniest thing to Ramsey, her hair flowed down her back which always made Ramsey question her ethnicity. Berta swore she was from an all-black southern stock, but Ramsey begged to differ. He didn't know any full blooded black girls with hair as naturally fine as Berta's. Strangely enough, although Berta was younger than Ramsey, she managed to somehow have a motherly effect on him.

"Berr-Breezy" yelled Ramsey. Berta smiled at the sound of Ramsey's voice and her nickname that only Ramsey called her. "Berr-Breezy" continued Ramsey, I need a big favor".

Berta just shook her head smiling to herself. Her partner hadn't even put the car in park yet and this fool was already asking for a favor. Berta loved and respected Ramsey. They'd worked a few homicides together and she got to see firsthand what all the hype about Ramsey was. And now she too knew it wasn't just hype.

"No, can do Ram. Caps got me on this triple homicide, I just came by to steal the Cap for a second. I need him to press Hein rich to get this warrant signed off on ASAP."

"You got a suspect already?" asked Ramsey

"Yes sir" smiled Berta as she exited the car.

"Then let your partner handle Furnari, I need you right now, bad."

"Sorry Ram, I'm taking this one by the horns." Berta spotted Furnari and made her way towards him. Ramsey quickly back peddled to keep up with Berta. The way he instinctively dodged a large stone one the lawn reminded Berta why she admired Ramsey so much.

"Look, you already got your case solved. Let the grunts do the grunt work" said Ramsey. Berta flashed Ramsey one of her infamous back off looks, but Ramsey wasn't budging. "I need all the help I can get wit this. Shit's braking and it's happening fast, if I don't get a hold of it now I may never catch this dude."

Berta stopped walking to consider helping Ramsey. Ramsey could see the wheels turning in her head as she thought. Berta's ambition was her drive as well as her weakness, and Ramsey played to that beat like an African percussionist.

"Not to take anything away from your triple, but this is a career making case right here. You know I don't give a fuck about moving up the ladder, who do you think I'm gonna give the credit to after I say Furnari's name" grinned Ramsey.

Berta resumed her walk to Furnari with Ramsey dead on her heels.

"Captain" started Berta "I've got the triple solved; I need Heinrich to get a warrant squeezed out like an hour ago."

"So get it" retorted Furnari. Furnari respected Berta, but he feared her more than anything else. She was too smart for her own good, and her ambition could be threatening in the future.

"I need your juice on this one Cap. The evidence is completely circumstantial, but I think I can crack one of them once I get'em in custody."

"No can do" answered Furnari. "I need to be here for any new developments."

"Nothing's happening here" interjected Ramsey. "Anything we find here won't be discovered until we get back to the lab. I mean it's not like cameras aren't following Berta's case, a kid got killed."

"And just what the fuck are you insinuating" growled Furnari.

"Nothing Cap" smiled Ramsey. "I'm just saying Jenkins case is as important as mines."

Furnari stared at Ramsey with pure contempt. God knows Furnari wanted to upstage Ramsey just once. "Are you sure about your suspect Jenkins?" asked Furnari

"Bout as sure as I am that Ramsey's a manipulative jerk."

With a smile Furnari placed his hand on Berta's shoulder, "let's go." Berta stepped back so quickly from Furnari's gesture he had no time to support the weight of his hand, causing it to drop suddenly.

"I can't go" said Berta. "That's why I need you to go. Hein rich would never sign off on a warrant like this for Greg, that's why I need you."

"And what the hell are you going to be doing?" snapped Furnari.

Ramsey quickly chimed in, "it might be something you're better off not knowing about sir. You know, like some off the record police work type shit," he chuckled.

Furnari was fed up with Ramsey, as Furnari made a step towards Ramsey Berta smoothly slid into the middle of them.

"Look Cap, times of the essence on this, we're going to be at this scene for hours, more like days. Let Ramsey do the grunt work, while you help me bring some closure to a grieving family." Berta blinked her big chestnut brown eyes at Furnari and instantly melted his heart.

Ramsey watched as the Captain's face changed from hardened asshole to kid who was just scolded by his mom in a way that made you still feel good. I guess I'm not the only one who looks at her like a mom, thought Ramsey to himself.

"Come on Cap, I'll walk you to the car and fill you in on the details" said Berta as she walked Furnari away.

Ramsey applauded Berta in his head. He watched her as she walked away. Damn Berta thought Ramsey to himself. Your ass is looking kind a fat in them jeans, and you slimming up. I might have to put something to that. Ramsey's thoughts were interrupted by his cellphone. Without looking at the caller id Ramsey answered the phone.

"Ramsey."

"What up nigga, fuck is you doin, we at the spot waitin for you."

"Be there in ten minutes yo."

"Yo if you can't make it, we got this shit dawg."

"Dread, don't fuckin play me, I said ten minutes."

"Whatever man, just hurry the fuck up. You remember how much longer we had to wait for another chance on this, all for that same stupid ass case."

"Kids are dying bro, are you fuckin serious."

"Fuck them kids, like I give a fuck about some cops kids, nigga I'd a kilt all them niggas twice for this type a bread nigga, fuck is you talkin bout kids died." Dread was breathing lightly into the phone waiting for Ramsey to respond.

"I'll be there" answered Ramsey right before he hung up on Dread.

"So where do we start first?" questioned Berta as soon as Ramsey ended his call.

"Berr-Breezy I hate to do this to you, but I gotta go."

"Are you fucking kidding me Ramsey?"

"Something's come up with one of my kids, look I just need you tonight, Kinkay knows exactly what I need you to do. Please Berr-Breezy?"

"You owe me three."

"Three! Goddamn Berr-Breezy. Fuck it, you got that."

Ramsey kissed Berta on the check and jogged away. Berta stood there a little flabbergasted. She knew Ramsey had something going on and she knew it wasn't his kids. She just prayed that he stayed safe. Back to work said Berta to herself as she snapped herself out of things that clouded the attention on the job.

"All right people" yelled Berta. I want this tape pushed back another ten feet, "and I need someone to find Dr. Kinkay now."

Ramsey hopped into his car and started to make a call as he drove away. The number Ramsey dialed went straight to voicemail so he left a message.

"Eagle Eye, Inferno, Officer Sloan, presumed dead."

Chapter 15

Ramsey arrived at the spot a little after midnight. The spot was located in Roxbury, smack dead in the middle of the projects. Dread paid a female crack head room and board for a two-bedroom apartment, allowing him to operate out of the project home under her name. They didn't go overboard with the spot but they made it enjoyable. A few 40' inch flat screen televisions mounted the walls linked to one entertainment system. A pool table graced the den along with a fully decked out bar with a beer tap.

Ramsey walked through the door only to be greeted by a cloud of weed smoke.

"It's the almighty Rah" sung Tommy as Ramsey walked in. "What up my Nig" said Tommy as he shook hands with Ramsey followed by a hug. Tommy was the life of the group. He was always smiling, always happy, and always joking. Tommy was tall and lanky, he stood at six foot six with a chipped front tooth. His hair was cut low with waves that looked like they were actually moving. Tommy's light green eyes and caramel skin made him "exotic" to girls from the neighborhood growing up, eventually the women as well. Tommy was flashy, which always concerned Ramsey, but Tommy also had a reputation for being a gigolo. Since they were young females just bought Tommy things or gave him money for no reason. Dread had encouraged Tommy to become a pimp but Tommy just wouldn't do it.

Ramsey never encouraged Tommy pimping for personal reasons, but deep down inside Ramsey knew Dread was right, Tommy was born to pimp. Tommy played his role in the group to a tee, staying in the finest clothes, expensive cars, manicures and pedicures weekly. Tommy was definitely a ladies man in every sense of the word. On the downside Tommy had children with three different women. Two of the women were sisters. None the less Tommy maintained a relationship with all his kids, their mothers, and a gang of girlfriends.

"Two-gun Tommy, what it do my dude?" replied Ramsey.

"Shit, what it do is we've been waitin on yo ass all fuckin night" said Dread as he walked over and embraced Ramsey in the same manner Tommy had.

"Where's Deebs?" asked Ramsey, ignoring Dread's ball busting remark.

"Inside man called him. He's in the bathroom talkin to him now" answered Tommy.

Suddenly Deebs burst out the bathroom, making a bee line straight for the weapons laid out on the kitchen table.

"Gotta go fellas" said Deebs as he put a bullshit .380 on his hip, followed by two clips and a nine millimeter made by smith and Wesson.

"What's good?" said Tommy as he joined his brother at the table and started loading up.

"Money's being moved now" responded Deebs. Deebs looked at Ramsey when he answered Tommy. Ramsey was at the table but hadn't touched a weapon.

Ramsey looked each individual at the table in the eye. Ramsey had openly expressed his concern about taking this job. The lack of information scared him, but his team was adamant about doing this job and chances of success only increased with Ramsey going along. Ramsey slowly picked up some off brand 38 and put it on his waist.

"Deebs, you're with me, you two stay close" was all Ramsey said as he turned and hustled out the front door.

"So what's happening Deebs?" asked Ramsey as he started the car.

"Seems like the cartel don't let 'em know when they movin the money" replied Deebs. "They was on stand by and got the call."

"So your guy is wit the money right now?"

"He just picked it up. He said he thought they was just makin a regular stop, turned out to be the pickup."

"You trust this muthafucka?"

"Bout as much as I trust anyone playin for another team."

"How's he gonna get another call to us?"

"I gave him that tracking device you told me to give 'em, and he already turned it on. They just hit Milton headed towards the ave."

"They comin through Pan?"

"Looks like it."

"And we don't know where the exchange is taking place?" questioned Ramsey with concern.

"Not a clue" sighed Deebs. Deebs knew where Ramsey was going with this. He knew Ramsey didn't like the lack of information going into this mission. But the fact still remained that there was over a five million dollars at stake, how could they not take a shot at it.

Chapter 16

Riding in another car behind them Dread smoked on a blunt filled with marijuana while rapping along to Lil Wayne's hit single "Duffel Bag Boy." Tommy bobbed his head quietly while sipping on his bottle of Remy Martin.

"Yeah if I wasn't police I'd be a fucking rapper yo" laughed Dread out loud.

"Nigga get the fuck outa hear" laughed Tommy.

"Naw for real yo I mean Rick Ross's fake ass did it. Granted he was a C.O and I'm real police, but dawg we more gooned up then any of them niggas. We got about 60 Street soldiers, we move more work than any crew in the city, and I ain't never testified at a trial a day in my life. (Laughing) Shiiiitt I might fuck around and be able to pull that shit off."

"You call Notty?" laughed Tommy as he pictured his best friend as some big time rapper.

"Shit let me call him now."

"Notty Damus a.k.a. shoot a nigga once a week a.k.a got the biggest Dick in the squad. Who this?

"Where the fuck you at?" Laughed Dread. Notty was Dread's number one street soldier. At 24 Notty was the wildest thing the streets could handle. Monster squad was the biggest gang on the rise in Boston and they were gaining momentum.

"I'm in the hood, what's good nigga?"

"Tool up, we headed your way."

"Aight yo," Notty, hung up the phone and turned to a kid no older than 12. "Tell Putt, Sin, and Swag-G to bring trick-or-treat around the corner."

The kid took off running. Notty leaned against the utility box and pulled out an empty pack of Newports. "Yo Reese let me get a bogey," demanded Notty.

Just then Swag-G, Putt, and Sin pulled up in trick-or-treat. Notty took the cigarette from Reese and jumped in the passenger seat.

"Head towards The Bury," ordered Notty as Swag-G pulled off.

Ramsey watched the tracking device, thinking about everything that could go wrong. He purposely let his job get in the way so he could cancel the first mission scheduled to steal the money. Even worse, they were using the Monster Squad for back up. Ramsey stayed out of the gang business as much as he could but Dread was neck deep into it. Dread was the man behind the man, the unspoken leader of Monster Squad.

Ramsey knew how bad Dread wanted all of them to quit the force and run the gang full-time, but Ramsey would never let that happen as long as he could help it. It wasn't so much quitting the force that Ramsey cared about. It was the amount of heat Monster Squad had generated. Monster Squad was on the Feds radar and Ramsey had no intentions of becoming an inmate. His final reason for not allowing the move was the control factor. As long as they remained cops Ramsey was H.N.I.C but if they were to go back to the streets 100% Dread would be the one calling the shots. Ramsey took nothing away from Dread, when it came to running a gang, Dread played his position better than most. Unfortunately, Dread had a temper, a temper that could compromise his judgment at the wrong time. Ramsey didn't have enough clout in the hood to override Dread, but in light of Dread's pressure and his growing urge for something new Ramsey was already putting contingency plans in place.

When they got out of Dorchester as kids Dread and Tommy went back to the hood every day with or without the knowledge of Captain Martin. Since birth Tommy, Dread and Deebs had been parented by Monster Squad which was still in its infancy stage. Deebs was the oldest at seven when Monster Squad was started, Tommy and Dread born a day apart making them both five and Ramsey smack dead in the middle at six.

Notty's older brother Monster had started the gang. It was easy for Monster to win over Deebs and Tommy, the lack of structure in their home left them defenseless to the allure of the streets. Tommy and

Deebs had different fathers but that never bothered their relationship growing up. Girls used to think Tommy was lying when he would say Deeds was his brother. Deebs wasn't too soft on the eyes but he had other qualities that made girls overlook that. Dread's dad was a Deacon in the church and his mother an Evangelist. Church folk in the hood used to say that the devil himself was trying to possess Dread because his parents were such devoted Christians. Ramsey did it alone, with no father and a mother whose past choices seemed to haunt them forever.

Chapter 17

When Dread, Deebs, Tommy, and Ramsey became persons of interest in a triple homicide their parents didn't know what to do. Captain Martin was the parent's knight in shining armor, getting the entire investigation brought to a halt. So when Captain Martin offered to take the four boys out of the hood and give them a fair shot at a real-life, their parents basically felt obligated to say yes.

Ramsey remembered the night of the murders like it was yesterday, he was fifteen Deebs had just turned sixteen and Dread and Tommy were fourteen. They were way across town in Mattapan inside another project rolling dice. It was seven of them total, a girl from the projects who lived in the building, and two drug dealers from another area. The plan to rob the two drug dealers was simple, roll craps for a few minutes then rob the two dealers while they were in the middle of rolling dice. Ramsey had used the girl from the projects to set the whole thing up.

Ramsey smoked a cigarette while Tommy rolled the dice.

"Seven nigga, gimmie that bread" screamed Tommy with laughter. Dread laughed with him.

"Damn nigga, you keep hittin like that, this nigga gonna be claiming bankruptcy" roared Dread.

"Bankrupt who?" replied the unsuspecting victim "you little niggas can't stay out long enough to break this bank. Fuck you got in the bank right now."

"Yo let's just bounce" said the victim's companion.

"2000," hollered Tommy "you tryin to stop it?"

"The banks stop for the next ten rolls little nigga" slick mouthed the victim.

"Fuck is all this little nigga shit about?" asked Deebs. Deebs was growing impatient with the robbery and he was really getting tired of being called little nigga.

"That's what you niggas is" responded the victim.

"Chill" said Ramsey to Deebs.

"Roll them shits" laughed Dread. Tommy rolled the dice. Seven, eleven, five, eight, four, five, ten, six, six, eight, ten, by his fourth win Ramsey thought to himself, shit if Tommy keeps rolling like this we won't have to rob these niggas. The victim was cursing and losing his cool all at the same time. He was losing his Re-up money to kids and he wasn't happy about it. He had just stopped by the projects to run a train on a project slut and then be about his business. The girl told them that she wanted to smoke before she fucked but they couldn't smoke in the apartment, so they went behind the building where these little motherfuckers were rolling dice and already smoking weed. So instead of getting some pussy he was losing all of his money to a bunch of kids.

Tommy shook the dice high in the air. If Tommy won, this roll the dealers would be broke. Tommy let the dice roll from his fingertips, his form couldn't be more perfect, his wrist curved like a professional bowler, his fingers snapped perfectly in rhythm with the releasing of the dice. The dice hit the wall, one dice bounce back and landed on a four. The other dice bounced into a nonstop spin. The victim's friend was fed up with him, he'd lost over half their re-up, and he wasn't about to let him lose it all. He was at the point where he was ready to kill somebody. In a rage he rushed over and kicked the spinning dice.

"Yo, what the fuck you do that for?" yelled Tommy.

"I stopped the dice nigga, I can do that."

"Fuck you mean" fired Dread, "you ain't even in the game."

"My money down there, fuck if I ain't in the game?"

"Naw fuck that" retorted Tommy "I won that roll you niggas owe thirty-two hundred."

"Fuck out a here" replied the friend "roll them shits."

"Naw Tommy, don't roll shit" said Dread

"Forget it Tommy" spoke up Ramsey "we'll just take our winnings and step"

"Fuck you" said the victim "niggas ain't gonna give me a chance to win my money back?"

"Your man over here cheatin" said Ramsey.

Suddenly the victim's friend pulled out **a** gun and pointed at Tommy.

"Gimmie this money nigga" said the friend as he snatched part of the money from Tommy. Deebs already saw how the situation was going to end when the victim's friend had kicked the dice. Deebs had quietly positioned himself on the blind side of the friend. Once the friend had pulled the gun to rob Tommy all hell really broke loose.

Deebs pulled a .44 from his waist line and fired a slug into the friend's torso. As the friend stumble back the victim tried to take off running. Tommy and Dread both pulled out .38 revolvers and let off every bullet they had. As mini sparks of fire emitted from both their guns, slugs took chunks of brick out of the wall while others slugs took chunks of flesh out of the victim's back. The victim's friend managed to return fire while stumbling back but his 9.mm was no match for Deebs' .44 at close range. Deebs fired three more shots hitting the friend twice.

The little girl from the project was frozen with fright, she had dropped to her knees and was covering her head from fear. Without thought the four of them with Ramsey bringing up the rear started to haul ass out of the back of the building. Ramsey stopped running long enough to observe the gruesome scene and made an executive decision.

Ramsey walked back over to the girl still crying with her head covered, pulled out a .25 and put two bullets in the girl's head. Afterwards he hustled over to both of the other victims and did the same thing to them. Ramsey wasted no time picking up the dice and the scattered money and ran out of the back of the building via another exit.

It was the murder of the little girl that sparked a never ending war between Monster Squad and the Still Ville projects. The death of the two drug dealers also brought problems from a local side street in Mattapan where the dealers were originally from. It was the beef with the Still Ville projects that got Monster killed, and it was at Monsters funeral that all four of them had sworn to be Monster Squad until they died.

Chapter 18

"Yo Ram" said Deebs

"What up, what up, we there?" questioned Ramsey who was caught up so deep in memory lane that he didn't notice they had stopped.

"Notty's here" replied Deebs

They were inside a parking lot at a McDonalds on Warren Street in Roxbury. The McDonalds was neighbored by an AutoZone, and a Sovereign Bank that was connected to a bunch of other stores along with a row of apartment buildings that lined up across the street.

First thing Ramsey noticed was trick-or-treat. The all black Dodge caravan glowed with its orange interior containing only a driver seat and a passenger seat. The van was driven on Boston streets for one reason and one reason only, extermination. This was the first time the van had ever been in a parking lot. For this mission the one cardinal rule pertaining to trick-or-treat would **be** broken. Rule number one; trick-or-treat only stops for five reasons, a red light, a stop sign, stupid ass pedestrians running across street, to let someone get out and shoot, and to just shoot. Rule number two: see rule number one. Ramsey personally came up with the rules for trick-or-treat, he wanted to give as little chance as possible to anyone seeing trick-or-treat or trick-or-treat being seen on camera. This particular trick-or-treat vehicle had already been used twice, three strikes and you're out thought Ramsey to himself. Ramsey watched Swag-G, Sin, and Putt jump out of the van.

Notty was the only one in his twenty's out of the group, Sin was nineteen, Putt was eighteen, and Swag-G was a fresh sixteen. All three had their qualities, Sin and Putt needed no instructions only targets to do what they specialize in.

People who rode on a trick or treat operation were specially trained by Deebs, Tommy, and Dread. Monster Squad members were given an opportunity most street level gangsters never had, which was proper training. Tommy and Dread had been on the force just a few years less than Deebs. Deebs went straight to narcotics while Tommy and Dread joined the S.W.A.T team. Dread took training his soldiers personally, and Sin and Putt had turned out to be elite force material. Notty on the other hand was a special breed. Notty was third-generation Monster Squad, but he was a part of the first generation ever to be trained. Notty's natural hate for human life seemed unreal. Along with remarkable aim and the heart of a lion. Notty was the uncontested heart beat and pride of Monster Squad and the heir to the throne. Swag-G was Notty's son, not his biological son but his son nonetheless. Swag-G had one specialty besides his style, driving cars. Swag-G had been stealing cars since he was nine years old and by the time he was thirteen he'd been in more high speed chases than the Dukes of Hazard. After his last getaway chase Ramsey indirectly convinced Dread to make Swag-G the sole driver for trick-or-treat.

Everyone embraced each other, Ramsey, not wanting to waste any time, got right to business.

"Okay, here's the drill, we're going with plan B, it's all we got so here's a quick recap. Me and Deebs pull over the car, if possible, hand cuff the vic take the money and leave. Complications, Dread and Tommy back us, trick-or-treat backs them. Trick-or-treat only gets involved if absolutely necessary. Understood?"

Notty and his companions all nodded and mumbled yes. Ramsey turned around and went back to his vehicle as did everyone else. Ramsey was nervous, he'd pulled heist like this before but never for this amount and never without a great plan in place. He just didn't know what to expect and he didn't like it.Deebs glanced over at his best friend, his younger but bigger homey. He could tell Ramsey was nervous, I'm not too excited about this plan either thought Deebs to himself, but with this much on the line how the fuck could we afford not to try. The only thing Deebs disagreed with Ramsey on was using trick or treat as extra backup. Dread had made a good point about why trick-or-treat was necessary, over five million dollars, the cartel, and a shady inside man, this was a recipe for a shootout with all the trimmings.

Chapter 19

"So where they at now?" asked Ramsey.

"Just passing Suns pizza shop headed up the ave"

"Aight we'll make a U-turn a few blocks up and get behind them. From there we'll observe the situation, assess, calculate, and then execute."

Swag-G turned up the AC in the van turned down the volume on the radio and then turned the radio on. Instinctively Notty smacked Swag-G in the back of the head.

"Damn nigga" whined Swag-G.

"Fuck you mean damn nigga, why the fuck is the music on?" Snarled Notty. Swag-G quickly turned the music off. It was Notty's rule that no music ever got played in trick-or-treat. Swag-G was the only reason why a radio was in trick-or-treat. When Swag-G had gotten promoted to be the sole driver for trick or treat he was amped until he sat inside the driver's seat, reached for a volume button where a radio should've been only to discover there was no car radio. Swag-G pleaded with Notty to put a radio in the car but Notty wouldn't budge on the rule, he said it was a distraction. Swag-G refused to drive and Dread had to get involved. Dread allowed Swag-G to put a sound system in with a few restrictions. Swag-G didn't care, he just needed to have the tools that helped allow him do what he did best.

"This shit is serious Swag-G, I need you on point" said Notty as if he regretted putting his hands on Swag-G which he did.

"Then let me do me" said Swag-G as he looked Notty defiantly in the face while turning the music back on.

If that were anyone else Notty would've disregarded his regret and put hands on that person again, but Swag-G was different. Notty didn't really care about the music anyway, he just wanted Swag-g to be on his super A game.

"Fuck is these niggas doin?" mumbled Swag-G out loud as he watched Deebs make a U-turn.

Putt bobbed his head as some old school Raekwon hummed through the speakers. Swag-G wasn't really into that era of music, but he played for Putt and Sin. Putt and Sin were the youngest old heads on the block. Damn near everything they did besides the way the dressed was like a nigga from the mid-nineties. Sin was in his own world as he bobbed to the tunes. Sin didn't know what the targets looked like, what was being taken, but what he did know was that if needed, the M-16 that rested in his lap would change any and all tides.

Chapter 20

"First side street we take we light em up?" hypothesized Deebs. Ramsey had already contemplated where the stop would take place. He knew he needed a quiet area in a loud inner city. Deebs always knew when Ramsey just thought of a solution. The lights in Ramsey's head would burn so bright you could see streaks of white flash across his pupils like mini bolts of lightning.

Ramsey pulled out his cell and phoned Dread. "Hit your lights and fly up to Columbia road. When I give you the signal be ready to force the traffic to head towards Franklin Park."

"For what?" asked Dread.

"Just do it" barked Ramsey.

"What about Notty?"

"We got it."

Dread threw on his lights and zipped by Ramsey and the target.

"Deebs, cut off trick-or-treat before they try to follow Dread" instructed Ramsey.

"Fuck is this nigga doin" said Swag-G as Deebs cut him off from following Dread.

Notty quickly picked up the audible, "fall back and follow Ram" replied Notty.

The Inside Man's heart skipped a beat when he saw the police lights in his rearview mirror. He thought Deebs was making his move. The Inside Man was nervous as hell, he had no idea the money was counterfeit until after he'd called Deebs. He hadn't had another opportunity to call Deebs again, not to mention the Mexican escort they picked up while on the highway headed to Boston. The Inside Man was so nervous beads of sweat were rolling down his forehead while the AC was on blast. He didn't even notice the change in the flow of traffic until the Passenger with him spoke.

"Why are they making us turn left?"

"Don't have the slightest clue" responded the Inside Man. The flow of traffic had been forced west at the intersection of Columbia Road and the entrance to Franklin Park, which was home to a nice side road that runs for about a half a mile. Lights flashed behind them while traveling on the side road. The Inside Man braced himself for change.

Ramsey and Deebs exited their car, Ramsey watched as trick-or-treat silently rolled by. Ramsey quickly prayed that everything went smoothly.

Deebs wanted his target secure before Ramsey asked the Inside Man for his license and registration so he quickly rushed the Passenger's door and demanded that he roll down his window. Ramsey had only made it to the middle of the Inside Mans trunk when a black

Mazda Ramsey and Deebs had made note of earlier pulled up to an abrupt stop. Deebs wasted no time and quickly drew his firearm, relieving his clip of two rounds.

Ramsey dove over the trunk of the Inside Man's car to get some cover for himself.

Dread and Tommy were already headed in the direction they had been steering traffic, but the sound of shots made the situation a hundred times more intense.

Ramsey drew his weapon. His mind was no longer pondering the 'what ifs', he was on auto pilot. His senses tweaked up a notch as gunfire being returned by the Mazda crashed medal and glass. Deebs rose to fire again only to be struck in the head by a bullet administered by the Passenger. Ramsey watched as Deebs fell, immediately over thirteen rounds went into the Passenger's door in a calculated pattern that guaranteed injury, hopefully in this case death.

Notty watched as Deebs hit the ground. The level of play had just hit reckless endangerment.

"Hell fuckin yeah" said Dread as he pulled up hard to the scene and placed the car in park. All he could see was fire emitting from the mac elevens wielded by three men crouched behind the Mazda he and Tommy had also marked earlier. He could see Ramsey taking cover behind the Benz that the target was in. Tommy exited the vehicle in a low crouch position, giving himself immediate cover. A fully automatic shotgun was slung over his shoulder while he gripped a .45 in his hands. Dread pulled an MP5 from under his seat as he exited the car, Tommy let off two rounds from his .45 to draw the gunmen's attention, followed by Dread with a volley of bullets.

"Deebs is hit" Ramsey yelled, but the gunfire drowned out his cries.

Swag-G skirted to a halt only yards away from the shootout, Sin and Putt hopped out with uncanny precision ripping their M16's at the assailants as they tried to reposition themselves from the gun fire Dread and Tommy were putting on them. Bullets ripped through the Mazda like a wet paper bag, traffic was in disarray as people tried to steer away from the mini war that was taking place in front of their eyes.

In a crouched position Tommy made a B line straight to the trunk of the Mazda while Putt and Sin were busy leaving no exit strategy. Dread kept the Mexicans from trying to run off into the park that lay behind them.

"Get right on that Benz Swag, we gotta help Big D out" instructed Notty

Swag-G was a tenth of an inch off the bumper of the Benz in seconds. Notty slid open the rear door facing Ramsey and jumped out.

Tommy could hear the Mexicans speaking in broken Spanish as he hunkered behind the trunk of the Mazda arming himself with his shotgun. Tommy waited to hear the sound of the M16's before he stepped from around the corner of the trunk and let off five rounds from his weapon. The shootout was over, Tommy raised his hand to signal for everyone to cease fire.

Dread made his way to the Inside Man's door while Tommy checked the dead Mexicans for Id's. Dread flew open the driver door and popped the trunk. There it was two black extra-large duffels bags. Dread checked the contents of both bag s and almost fainted at the sight of all those Benjamin's staring at him.

"Got it" yelled Dread as he made his way around the Benz toward Ramsey. "Oh shit, Deebs is hit?"

"Deebs is what?" asked Tommy as he rounded the trunk only to see Ramsey pressing against Deebs' head trying to stop the bleeding.

"Notty get the bags out of here" ordered Ramsey. Putt and Sin were already putting the bags in the car as Notty made his way back to trick-or-treat. In seconds they were speeding off headed back to their neighborhood, which only happened to be a few blocks away.

Chapter 21

The stash spot for trick-or-treat was in Mattapan, another borough outside of Monster Squad territory. Swag-G made his way towards their hood, which was only a few blocks away from the massacre they'd just left behind. Notty noted how Swag-G maneuvered trick-or-treat like he was the lone rider on a brand new Kawasaki bike. The music was blaring out of the van as Swag-G weaved through oncoming traffic.

"What you want me to do with trick-or-treat?" asked Swag-G to Notty as he pulled away.

"Can't stash her on the block" offered Putt. "Too many people watchin us get up outa here"

"Get trick-or-treat to the Pan" said Notty. Putt, and Sin exited the car with the money and the guns.

Swag-G pulled off of Esmond Street and was so distracted with what just happened he didn't even notice the flashing blue lights behind him. Swag-G slowed down a bit, he had only made it a few feet down Esmond and he wasn't sure if he was the one being pulled over. Oh shit said Swag-G said to himself as he remembered Notty had just replaced the old police scanner with some shit that seemed like it was from the future. Since Esmond was a small one-way side street, Swag-G was able to appear as if he were looking for a place to pull over. Swag-G turned on the scanner just in enough time to hear trick-or-treat being described over the scanner and being pursued. Swag-G laughed out loud.

"We ain't in pursuit yet muthafucka" yelled Swag -G over the music.

Swag-G was now approaching the middle of Esmond where he was allotted some more space. The middle of Esmond Street turns into T where you could take a left onto Bradshaw or continue down Esmond. Thank God for this hemi engine and this hand e-brake I put in this muthafucka thought Swag-G. Swag-G mashed the pedal and spilled onto the other side Esmond.

With blue and white lights flashing dead on his tail Swag-G banged hard on the wheel with a left turn while pulling up his e-brake. Swag-G could only hope his timing and spacing was perfect as he quickly straightened out the wheel. Swag-G had attracted several other cop cars, and he was now facing the cops that were just on his bumper. Swag-G's move was so unexpected that the cops racing behind one another down Esmond almost crashed into each other making the right off of Bradshaw. With no time to waste Swag-G floored it up the one way, back up Esmond Street. Swag-G flew up the one way knowing if he hesitated one time he would crash.

The unmarked detective car hit the corner of Esmond so fast and hard that the detective behind the wheel had no reaction time for the oncoming black van. The driver was a mystery due to the fact that the front window had a smoked tint. Detective Wyles thought for sure they were going to collide.

Fuck thought Swag-G as the all grey D-boy car hit the corner at top speed. Don't think, just make a decision is all that ran through Swag-G's head as he banged the hardest right of his life into the last driveway only a few feet away from the apartment buildings that cornered Esmond Street. Swag-G knew a right at this speed would tip the van, he calculated the rear driver side of trick-or-treat slamming into the front of a truck that bordered the driveway. The impact stabilized trick-or-treat as Swag-G slammed her into reverse. The wheels burned as they revved into the opposite direction. Swag-G had a sixty-year-old Mexican for a mechanic who tricked out trick-or-treat with so many features you'd think Swag-G was a ghetto James Bond. One feature was the ability to go from drive to reverse without impacting the engine. The detective didn't react fast enough and screeched past the driveway. Swag-G was speeding off onto Blue Hill Avenue before the cops knew they should be reversing. Instead of taking the right onto Blue Hill Avenue, Swag-G expertly fought through traffic, taking a slight left onto Blue Hill Avenue, only to hit a hard right onto American Legion Highway and off towards Mattapan.

Chapter 22

Michael lay in a queen sized bed covered in red silk sheets. Shiny Oakwood post with beautifully carved baby cherubs to mount them cornered all four sides of the bed. He checked his wrist watch, only a couple of hours had passed since he left the bar to come home with Heaven. Glimpses of the home he'd driven to started to flash inside his mind. He'd drank with Heaven in the living room far past his limit. Everything from there was a blur for Michael, except the sex. It was the most intense sex Michael had ever experienced. It was like Heaven knew every inch of his body, where to touch and when to touch it. It was as if they had connected beyond the physical.

Michael rolled out of bed, and took a second to take in his surroundings. The room looked like it was a Hollywood set for a sex scene, dominatrix style with a whole lot of class. Fresh white and red roses adorned the entire room, red wallpaper with pictures of black figures both male and female in all different types of sexual positions. The room had a sweet lilac and honey smell to it. Michael made his way to his clothes that had been neatly folded on all black suede leather love seat. Michael quickly got dressed and ready with the intentions of leaving, but he couldn't remember which door led where, Heaven had like four different doors. Finally, Michael just picked a door and headed towards it.

Wrong door Mikey.

Michael walked from the door he was facing and headed east across the room. The hallway was dressed with countless paintings, the size of the hallway alone made Michael estimate the house to be at least seven figures. Michael was completely lost, to many doors and to many pictures.

"We're in the kitchen Michael."

Michael did a complete 360.

What are you a fuckin ballerina now?

Michael had heard Heaven's voice, but it wasn't like when you hear someone calling out to you from afar, Michael was hearing Heaven from inside his own head.

"Just come out, take a left at the end of the hallway and take the elevator to K."

My how the tides have changed.

Michael did as he was instructed, he was confused, but for some reason he felt stronger, his blood seemed to pump harder. He thought he was losing his mind. The elevator ride gave him a funny feeling, the classical music that played in the background was frightening more than it was soothing.

When the elevator stopped the doors opened to a luxurious living room. Famous paintings lined the walls, cathedral ceilings gave the room a larger than life feeling. The fire place roared as a woman dressed in a maid's attire dusted a lamp. The woman looked up at Michael, smiled and continued working. From out of an entrance to the left two men walked into the room. Michael was still a little foggy headed, so where he knew the men from he couldn't remembered.

"Why Marr we have a guest."

"Indeed we do Matt, let's introduce ourselves."

Matt and Marr scurried over to Michael.

"I sir go by the name Matt" said Matt with an extended hand. Michael shook Matt's hand, still bewildered by his environment. "And this is my best mate Marr" continued Matt as Marr extended his hand.

"Quite a grip on this fellow, wouldn't you say Matt?"

"Quite, so what's your name my good friend?" questioned Matt.

Suddenly Heaven walked in holding a cup of steaming coffee on a saucer. "Are these two scallywags bothering you Michael?" asked Heaven with heavy sarcasm in her voice.

"Why of course not" said Matt in an appalled voice.

"Why would you even say such a dreadful thing" whined Marr.

Heaven eyed Matt and Marr suspiciously before handing Michael his cup of coffee and taking a seat.

"Don't pay them any mind Michael, they're just troublemakers" said Heaven as she pulled Michael down to sit next to her.

Michael sipped his coffee, he wished the Voice would speak to him, instruct him or something.

'Don't be scared Michael.'

Michael jumped up crashing the coffee to the floor. "How are you doing that" yelled Michael.

Hey tuts why don't you put that fuckin mutt of a bitch of yours on a leash.

What's wrong Voice, your pet can't handle himself?

First of all Bitch its "The Voice", second of all its "The Voice" bitch.

"Ok Michael I'm sorry" replied Heaven. She gently rubbed his hand, "I'm sorry ok? It won't happen again."

"Fuck the apologies" retorted Michael. "How are you speaking in my head?"

"Just relax and have a seat, everything will be explained in good time" said Heaven.

Michael sat back down, wishing he still had his coffee, its warmth and strong taste calmed his nerves. Michael then realized where he remembered Matt and Marr from, they were the two guys at the bar whistling. Michael still couldn't get the fact that Heaven had a voice as well out his mind. He wondered if Matt and Marr had voices as well.

He questioned if they all had different voices or if it was the same one talking to them all.

Heaven could hear Michael's thoughts through Seduce, Michael's nervousness concerned them both. Heaven rubbed Michael's leg in a motherly manner than that of a lover. The maid appeared with a fresh cup of coffee.

"Look Michael" started Heaven "why don't you let me have some food prepared for you, afterwards you can shower and then I can show you L.A."

"No, what I want is to know is what the hell is going on. Who are you people?"

"I'll explain during the course of our night, how's that sound Michael?"

Sounds like you need some hearing lessons.

Now, now The Voice let the children play.

Heaven smiled as Michael relaxed and continued to sip his coffee. "So what would you like to eat?" asked Heaven.

"Some eggs and toast" replied Michael.

"Suela" said Heaven to the woman Michael saw dusting earlier. "Eggs and toast please."

Suela quickly scurried off. Her frumpy frame bounced pass Michael and Heaven in a blur.

"There's a shower down the hall, I'll go prepare it for you with a change of clothes. You look about Marr's size, he has a blazer that would like great on you" said Heaven as she rose to her feet. "Once dressed I'll have Charles warm up the Ferrari" declared Heaven in sort of a not an option tone. Heaven gently and ever so sweetly kissed Michael on the cheek and literally glided out of the living room and down the hall.

Chapter 23

Suela brought in a fresh cup of coffee, along with a plate of toast and some butter on the side.

"And how would you like your eggs sir?" the R's rolled off her tongue with a deep Mexican accent.

"Sunny side up, pepper, no salt please" replied Michael.

Suela curtly nodded her head and quietly stepped out of the room. Matt and Marr crept back into the room, making comical gestures as if they were making sure they weren't being watched. Matt jumped over the couch on Michael's right side while Marr slid in from the left.

"So where you from mate?" asked Marr

"Boston" answered Michael.

"Boston! Why I love Boston. Such culture and history, why I and Marr just visited there about a year ago" said Matt.

"Yes, delightful place. So what brings you west my good boy?" asked Marr.

"Ok, why do you guys talk like Brit's? It's obvious your accents are fake so what the fuck is your deal?" blurted Michael.

Matt and Marr smiled at Michael and then at each other from ear to ear. The way they talked was a private joke, linked back to their first kill during their college years.

'Oh don't mind us" chuckled Matt.

"Yes, please don't" chimed in Marr. "It's just a little college humor, from our golden years."

"Golden years, you guys don't look a day over 30."

"So what did you do in Boston?" asked Marr

"I was a police officer."

"A police officer, you must have hundreds of stories" replied Matt.

"Not really just a uniform cop."

"Why uniform cops see the most" retorted Marr.

"Oh I do agree" injected Matt.

"First on the scene" fired Marr

"Last to leave" flowed Matt.

"Well, I mean I've seen my share of shit but for the most part my job is like a rerun of cops. Drunks, dealers and suspended license's" shrugged Michael.

"Any hobbies?" shouted out Marr

"Or addictions?" slid in Matt

These fairies sure do ask a lot a fuckin questions.

Michael chuckled. 'Naw man, no addictions, I like to read, write, play football with my boys" Michael paused. "My boys" repeated Michael, in a whisper. Michael was frozen in time as images of Michael Jr. and Seth eclipsed everything in the room. Water welled in Michael's eyelids, as pain secreted from his heart and remorse bled from his soul.

"So you have children?" piped Marr

"Any pictures of the strapping lads?" asked Matt.

"No" choked out Michael. "No pictures, you'll have to excuse me for a second" said Michael rising.

Matt and Marr didn't miss a beat as they rose with Michael.

"What about breakfast?" asked Marr.

"Yes, you must eat."

"I know you're probably famished."

"Heaven can be quite exhausting" ended Matt.

Just then Suela walked back into the room with two sunny side up eggs, lightly sprinkled with pepper, along with another fresh cup of coffee.

"Thank you Suela" offered Marr

"Yes thank you, thank you very much" said Michael.

Suela politely bowed her head and exited the room.

"Lovely woman, don't you agree?" said Marr to Michael.

"I don't know, I guess so" answered Michael.

"Well her service and cooking skills are definitely unsurpassed. Go ahead, eat, make me a liar" said Matt.

Michael took a bite of his eggs, and he'd be damned if it wasn't the best pair of eggs he'd ever tasted. And come to think of it, he couldn't remember the last time he had a better tasting cup of coffee. The expression on Michael's face said it all.

"Ahh looks like we have another convert" gleamed Marr.

Heaven walked back into the room, somehow, with no change in her appearance Heaven managed to look more beautiful than she did the first time she left the living room.

"Away with you hyenas" joked Heaven. "Let the man eat in peace."

Matt and Marr both rose to their feet with sad childlike faces.

"You never let us have any fun" whined Marr.

"Never "finished Matt as he and Marr stomped out of the living in a comical manner of rage.

Chapter 24

Michael stood in the shower allowing the water to refresh his body and mind. Ever since he met Heaven it was as if time itself was slowing down, while life was speeding up. Nothing was adding up anymore, Michael didn't feel balanced, but for whatever reason Michael felt at one with Heaven. He was thrown off by these strange characters, the expensive furniture and the endless multimillion dollar paintings that seemed strewn all over the palace. A hot shower was just what he needed.

Once he was done showering and getting dressed Michael did a spot check in the mirror. Michael wasn't too fond of the blazer Heaven picked out, so he rummaged through the closet a little. Michael found a cream polo sweater that fit him perfectly. Suela walked up to the open door of the bedroom Michael was dressing in and knocked.

"Ms. Heaven is in the car waiting Senor."

"Lead the way senorita" smiled Michael.

Michael followed Suela down the hall towards another elevator that awaited them. Michael and Suela rode the elevator in silence. Dreadful classical music filled the space between Suela and Michael.

Will somebody shut this shit off?

Suela pressed a button turning off the elevator music only seconds before the elevator stopped.

"Your stop senor."

Michael glared suspiciously at Suela before stepping off the elevator.

"Hasta luego senor" smiled Suela as the elevator doors closed.

Did she turn the music off, or was it just the elevator stopping?

"You asking me?" replied Michael aloud.

Michael stepped into a fourteen car garage, the place looked like a mini car showcase. Everywhere Michael looked he saw Prancing Stallions, Bulls, huge B's, and backwards E's attached to B's. The stars lighting the sky gave a different type of light to the cars as their brightness streamed in from the glass ceiling.

Never judge a book by its cover Mikey, everything that glitters isn't gold.

"I think we hit the jackpot."

Somebody hit the jackpot.

You again?

Heey boo.

Heaven revved the engine to a Bloody Mary red Ferrari. The two door horse of fire glowed as a beam of light from a single star bounced just right off the glass, making the emblem appear life like. Heaven's crimson red scarf and Dolce and Gabbana shades made her look like a drop dead gorgeous southern bell as she sat behind the wheel of this roofless stallion.

Michael walked over to the passenger side and tilted his head ever so slightly to the right as he took in Heaven's undeniable beauty before entering the car. Heaven's natural red hair seemed to burn with the energy of an out of control fire. Heaven managed to wrap sophisticated, educated, classy, and sexy into a paradox of slutty out of control passion.

My, my, someone sure is smitten by you.

"Yeah" I think I'm a little smitten myself.

I reckon I can't blame you dear, but don't get too fond of him, there's something different about this one.

Heaven reveled in Michael's infatuation with her. Planning on taking full advantage of the situation Heaven put a little bounce in her flirt.

"What're you staring at silly?" giggled Heaven in an innocent and slightly embarrassed manner.

"N-n-n-nothing" stammered Michael.

That was smooth, did you teach him that line yourself The Voice? Can't I just call you Voice? The Voice just doesn't flow when used in certain contents. How about I call you V?

How about I have Michael rip Heavens fucking throat out?

"Well what you waitin for Tiger, jump in" said Heaven to Michael

He's certainly most welcomed to try.

"You didn't like the jacket?" frowned Heaven.

"Not my style, so where are we headed?" responded Michael coolly after finally regaining the composure he'd lost since he met Heaven.

Chapter 25

The Ferrari moved through the streets like a banshee. Heaven drove like a NASCAR driver mixed with a demolition derby demon. Heaven took unnecessary risk in the streets like she had some sort of death wish. Michael couldn't even exhale until they made it to the open road. Once they hit the open road it seemed like all the other cars disappeared. It was if Michael, Heaven, and the water were the only things that existed.

"So tell me Michael, how long have you been with your voice?"

Michael was stunned by the question; he didn't know if he should answer her or not.

"Oh don't be shy Michael. I've been with mines for over two decades now. Matt and Marr are young but they're coming along nicely."

I knew it Michael thought to himself, they do have voices.

"Well?" badgered Heaven.

"My-my whole life, well as least as long as I can remember."

"Now that's impressive."

"Why's that?"

"Well to be a killer from infancy takes a different breed of human don't you think?"

"Killer! Who said anything about being a killer?"

"How else do you think you obtained your Voice silly? It's only through the shedding of blood does one get bestowed with such an honor."

"Well I guess I'm an exception to the rule because I've never killed anyone." Although Michael was intrigued by Heaven's words, he had no intention of admitting to murder.

"Never committed murder" chuckled Heaven. "So what would you call all those family barbecue's, playing house? Or what about your wife and kids Michael, was that not murder?"

Michael instantly grew hot with rage, his insides burned like someone had poured a bottle of acid down his throat straight to his stomach.

"Stop the car" demanded Michael.

"Excuse me."

"Stop the car now."

Heaven quickly pulled the car over. Michael jumped out and stormed towards the water. It was as if the calming sway of the water was beckoning him. The uncontrollable rage that surged through

Michael seemed to grow stronger as he drew closer to the calming waves. Michael picked up some pebbles out of the sand and tried skipping them along the water. Every bounce caused a different ripple in time that displayed images of Michael and his family. Tears ravished Michael's cheeks as he thought about his wife and boys. Michael had always imagined himself growing old with Candice, being a grandfather and cursing out his grandsons for mischief, and chastising his granddaughters for being fast. Michael had truly loved Candice, he loved her more than anyone in the world. Michael was so deep in thought he didn't notice Heaven walk up behind him. The touch of her hand startled him.

"It's okay Michael" said Heaven as Michael flinched form her surprise touch. "Michael you have so much to learn. You could do great things Michael, you could become richer and stronger than you could ever imagine. Let me help you Michael, let me teach you how to harness the true power of your voice."

Michael stared out into the ocean. Heaven's words were a foreign language to him at this point. Michael felt alone, all his life he had The Voice to tell him what to do when he was lost. At a time like this Michael would've been yearning to hear from The Voice, but now all he could do was fiend for Candice's touch. Candice was the only person Michael could trust more than The Voice, because Michael could confide in Candice. At that moment Michael felt like just giving up. He wanted to just walk towards the water and never stop walking.

"Don't think like that Michael" pleaded Heaven. You have to much potential, Candice could never"

Before Heaven could finish her statement Michael wrapped his hand around her throat.

"As long as you live and breathe never mention her name again" snarled Michael through clenched teeth.

"I I I can't can't breathe Mi Michael."

Michael squeezed harder, bringing Heaven to her knees. Darkness began to collapse around her.

"Never again, are we clear?"

In a final desperation Heaven flailed her arms and nodded her head yes as much as she could.

That's my dawg, that's my dawg (sang The Voice)

Michael left Heaven on her knees and made his way back to the car.

Fiery one isn't he.

He sure is agreed Heaven.

Chapter 26

The ride along the coast wasn't tension filled, but it was quiet.

So he likes to put his hands on women I see.

You damn right, he could've been a pimp.

Naah, not enough ice in his veins for that.

Michael found himself in deep thought. He tried his best not to think because he knew Heaven could read his thoughts but it was too difficult not to think. So many different questions were running through Michael's head he couldn't focus on just one, he hadn't even noticed when the car came to a complete stop.

"So is it going to be Chinese, French, or Italian?" asked Heaven.

Michael looked slowly around, taking in the life of the downtown area. He didn't even know what city he was in. Michael watched as people shuffled in and out of bars, while other people stood in extensively long lines waiting to get into some club or restaurant. No one Michael observed seemed modest in the least. Fashion reigned supreme in this area with large bank accounts as a consigliore. Every sign Michael read was in any language other than English.

I guess a burger is out of the question.

Have some class for a change will you.

I wasn't born with class; I was born an American.

A patriot are we know (Heaven chuckled). Please, honor us with one of your best renditions of the Star Spangled Banner The Voice.

"Wow, whatever happened to a good old American cheeseburger."

"Don't be such a hill Billy Michael, how about Chinese. I know a place that makes an orange duck that is simply to die for."

"Whatever you say senorita, lead the way."

Heaven pulled in front of a restaurant simply titled Lo Kim. Heaven waited patiently until one of the valet boys stopped running their mouth long enough to notice her.

"Sorry about that mam" huffed the attendant as he opened Heaven's door.

"Are you new here?" questioned Heaven with a hint of disgust in her voice as she exited the car.

"Y-yes, yes I am."

"Word of advice from a regular to this fine establishment, instead of being sorry you should be attentive, hence the job title valet attendant."

Heaven proceeded to the front entrance with her arm looped through Michael's. The line for Lo Kim was around the corner and moving at a snail's crawl.

Look at the fucking wait on this line Mikey, go somewhere else.

Line, wait, only peasants wait or stand in line.

"Can we go somewhere else; I don't feel like waiting?"

"Wait" laughed Heaven in disbelief. "Michael you are so funny" Heaven continued to laugh as she escorted him to the front door parallel to the line.

"I'm sorry mam but the wait is going to be about another fifteen minutes" spoke the Marti D at the door to a couple getting impatient.

"Fifteen minutes!" yelled the blonde haired man. "We have reservations."

"As does everyone else behind you sir, but I am terribly sorry the situation is beyond my control" replied the Marti D.

"Usually when a restaurant books a reservation, it means they are reserving a time and a space for someone" snipped the black long haired woman that was with him.

Before the Marti D' could respond Heaven appeared with Michael by her side.

"Giles!!" gleamed Heaven to the Marti D.

"Ms. Heaven, so wonderful to see you, and who might this handsome devil be?" winked the Marti D.

"Just call him my new desert. I see business is doing well, is Mr. Kim in tonight?"

"I regret to inform you he is not my dear. He's attending the opening of a new Lo Kim in San Francisco."

"What a shame we missed him, oh well send him my love. I'll start with the usual" finished Heaven as she ushered Michael into the restaurant.

"What the fuck was that!!" screamed the blonde haired man.

"What was what sir?"

"That! We've been waiting for over twenty minutes and she just barges in."

"Who Ms. Heaven?"

"Who the fuck is Ms. Heaven!!"

"Why Ms. Heaven is, well, she's Ms. Heaven."

"And what're we? Sacks of meat?"

"Why of course not sir, I'm"

"You know what, fuck you and your fucking fortune cookies."

The couple stomped away to the words of the Marti D expressing that they don't sell fortune cookies.

"Was that Brad Pitt and Angelina Jolie?" asked Michael.

"Yes it was, and if you ask me their attire was a complete disgrace to lo Kim. That's probably why Giles gave them such a hard time."

As Heaven and Michael seated themselves a frail male Asian brought them a bottle of chilled Vin De Constance. Heaven ordered in Chinese giving Michael a wink when she was finished.

"Jack of all trades I see" replied Michael.

"More like a queen Michael more like a queen."

Chapter 27

Ramsey sat next to Deebs as Deebs laid in a coma. The sun was finally starting to break the grip of night. Ramsey was in a complete state of shock. His best friend, his protector, his brother, was in danger of never waking up. The doctors said chances were slim on Deebs recovering from his coma. Ramsey hadn't left Deebs side since the ambulance ride. No doctors could budge him and no detectives could question him. Deebs wife had wept in Ramsey's arms from the moment she made it to the hospital. Desirae was like a sister to Ramsey, she knew Ramsey needed to hold someone just as much as she did.

Outside of his emotional episode with Desirae, Ramsey was just as lifeless as Deebs. Every beep from Deebs' EKG machine was like the sound of someone shoveling dirt. Tommy and Dread had stopped by but Tommy couldn't stand to see his big brother like that.

Ramsey was lost in a sea of thoughts, waves crashed back and forth to quickly for him to analyze anything. The governor and mayor had already been by to see Deebs. Surgery was currently impossible; the bullet was in a critical position that put Deebs at great risk. The sea of nieces and nephews crying in the hallway only weakened Ramsey's strength. The real shocker was the community presence, which in hind sight only made things worse. Deebs was so loved by the streets real live gangsters were at the hospital showing support of his recovery. No one in Monster Squad visited the hospital via direct order from Notty, but that didn't stop other people from other neighborhoods throughout the city from showing up. Deebs was the reason for a lot of peace within the city, his situation was catastrophic on so many different levels that he had no choice but to pull through.

Ramsey's phone rang, jarring him out his coma like state.

"Ramsey. Yo it's Dread."

"What up yo."

"Berta's been assigned the case, she tried to interview me and Tommy>"
"What ya'll do?"

"Fuck you think we did nigga. Anyway, what up wit the big homey?"

"No change" replied Ramsey just as Berta walked into the room. "Yo let me holla at you later bro" finished Ramsey as he hung up on Dread.

"So how's he doing?" asked a truly concerned Berta.

"Not good, doctors said recovery is minimal."

"Fuck Ramsey, how could you be so sloppy?"

"What are you talking about?"

"Cut the shit Ramsey, Johnson and Jackson lawyered for good reasons. You, you better be fucking straight with me from the first word out of your got damn mouth."

Ramsey looked deep into Berta's eyes, and behind the fire in her words all he could see was grief. Berta placed her hands on Ramsey's. He knew Berta had a different kind of love for Deebs. When someone puts their own life at risk to saves yours you love them from a different part of the mystery that make us human. Ramsey wanted to be straight up with Berta, so he did the only thing he could do, Ramsey removed his hands from Berta's and turned away.

"Well just so you know the case is no longer mines. The feds picked it up. Supposedly the passenger in the Benz was an informant helping make a bust on the cartel. They also found about ten thousand dollars' worth of counterfeit money on the driver. That's all I know."

The feds thought Ramsey; this shit just went from turn in your badge bad, to inmate ID worse. Ramsey's super brain was processing so much data that this new bit of information put his processor in sleep mode. Too much was going on at one time, to many variables being added mid equation, his mind needed to rest.

"Berrr-Breezy, you mind hanging out with the big guy for a while?"

"Be my pleasure Ram"

"Thanks," replied Ramsey as he rushed past Berta.

Berta stopped Ramsey mid stride "you be careful Ramsey."

Ramsey looked at Berta, nodded his head and made his way out of the hospital room. Ramsey's computer restarted automatically. The Inside Man had counterfeit money, so chances are all of the money was counterfeit. Did the Inside Man know the money was fake? Did the Passenger know it was fake? Neither answer held consequence since both men were dead. The information was shredded. Did the feds know the money was fake? Were the feds tied to the fake money? Before Ramsey could compute the number of possibilities he was flanked by two men in dark colored suits.

"Detective Ramsey," spoke the taller male as he reached for Ramsey's arm. "FBI detective, please come with us."

Chapter 28

"Look, I've got nothing to say to you guys" started Ramsey. "So either charge me with something or get the fuck out of my face right now." Ramsey found himself sitting in a dark blue Crown Victoria in between the two feds who approached him in the hospital.

"Well since I want you to listen, not talking should make understanding what I have to say that much easier" stated the passenger of the car who never bothered to turn around. "Over five million dollars was stolen tonight and I want it back. I don't care how you do it detective, in twenty-four hours I want the money returned to a location we'll disclose to you once you've called with the money. If the money is not returned in twenty-four hours, you, detective Jackson, and the Johnson brothers" chuckled the man "will have a lot more than a prison cell to worry about."

For the first time the man in the passenger seat turned around. His inner being was hidden by a dark pair of unlabeled Gucci shades. He removed his shades to reveal a pair of ice cold gray eyes that only complimented his full white hair. The man appeared to be in his forties and in a decent shape as well.

"This is where you say yes, detective" finished the man.

Ramsey continued to look white hair in the face, not at all impressed with what he saw. Ramsey then observed the two men sitting on his left and right. Ramsey didn't recognize anyone in the car, no one even looked familiar and Ramsey had been dealing with almost every fed in the city now.

"Mind if I see some badges?" asked Ramsey.

Charcoal gray responded by putting a stiff elbow into Ramsey's gut. Ramsey instantly buckled over, the blow was so sudden and with no time to brace Ramsey could do nothing but keel over. Ramsey's first instinct was to break Charcoal Gray's face but he thought it wiser to play it weak. Besides, Ramsey now knew that these guys were about as FBI as the man who pan handled in the middle of Blue Hill Avenue.

"Twenty-four hours' detective" repeated the white haired man while tossing Ramsey a cheap twenty-dollar virgin mobile cellphone. "Call the number in the contact list when you have it."

Charcoal Grey got out of the car so Ramsey could be shoved out. Ramsey still managed to get the license plate as the Crown Victorian swerved off into traffic. Not needing new problems on his plate Ramsey quickly began to contain the situation.

"Sanders" answered the man who Ramsey had called.

"Yo Jeff it's me Ramsey."

"Shit Ram, the feds are here right now ripping your desk apart. They going through all ya files, this shit is crazy bro."

"Look, fuck all that, I need you to run a plate for me. Delta, Bravo, Sierra, 9, 5, 2. Call me back when you got something."

"Alright, I'll call you back in a sec." said Jeff as he hung up.

Seconds later Ramsey was calling Dread. "Where you at?"

"I'm at the spot, why what up?"

"Get Tommy and don't move, we need to meet" answered Ramsey before hanging up.

Ramsey's phone rang as soon as he hung it up. The ringtone chimed a tune set for one person only.

"I think you need to come see me" said the voice on the line before the line went dead.

Ramsey hustled his way to his car, the last thing he needed was a sit down, but they never hurt either. Ramsey's phone rang again; it was only Furnari so Ramsey let it go to voicemail. His phone rang again as he pulled off to meet special ringtone.

"Jeff! What you got for me?"

"Not much Ram, the car was a rental. Some guy named Jeffrey Blair used a credit card from a company called European Rugs."

"Find out what you can about that company for me and get it to me yesterday."

"Are you ok Ram?"

"I got the feds going through my shit, my best friend is in a fucking comma, no, I'm not ok Jeff. Can you just get this done for me?"

"Call you as soon as I get something Ram."

"Thanks."

"Hey Ram."

"What up."

"Be careful."

Ramsey hung up the phone, shit was past being careful. The situation in front of Ramsey was spinning out of control but he still felt he had a grip on things. Ramsey needed to tighten the grip, rather than let things continue to develop to a point too big for his control to contain. Without knowing he was there, Ramsey pulled into Special Ringtone's driveway.

Chapter 29

The meeting with Special Ringtone didn't go as Ramsey would've liked it, but nonetheless a solution had been formed. Ramsey didn't care about giving the money back, it was not retaliating for Deebs that didn't sit well with him. But the decision was made, a war with the mob was the last thing they needed. Ramsey knew this wouldn't go over well with Dread, and the mere thought of looking Tommy in the eye and telling him to leave it alone made Ramsey cringe. No one in Monster Squad would understand the ruling, and no one but Ramsey had the calculated mind to make them understand.

Ramsey pulled up to the spot, he could hear the music blazing from the apartment as he paralleled parked. Ramsey walked into the apartment to see Dread and Tommy sitting in opposite chairs getting their dicks sucked by two neighborhood hood rats. The girls both jumped up, startled by Ramsey's entrance.

"That's just my nig bitch" slurred Tommy. "Now get back on this dick."

"Actually ladies" stated Ramsey. "You need to go" finished Ramsey as he stepped out of the way of an already open door.

"Ya'll bitches get outta here" yelled Dread.

The women quickly rose to their feet, grabbed their belongings and scurried out of the apartment. Tommy and Dread fixed their pants as Ramsey walked over to the bar and made himself a glass of Remy Martin. One would think, how anyone could think of engaging in a sexual act when their loved one had just been violently turned into vegetable only hours ago. But Ramsey knew what he was seeing was a very bad sign. A sexual act was the only thing that could keep Tommy and Dread from strolling into anyone of the local South Boston bars where known mob associates hung out and killing everything with a pulse.

"So who dies first?" questioned Dread as he rifled a round into a brand new AK47.

Tommy stood silently as his 50 Cal rifle hung from his shoulders. Tommy was the number one sniper on the entire east coast, according to him it was like watching someone die in a movie. All Ramsey could see when he looked at Tommy was Deebs. If the roles were reversed could he tell Deebs to stand down on Tommy being laid up in the hospital. The thought penetrated Ramsey's voice box every time he tried to speak the words.

"As soon as we secure our families, we kill everything associated with tonight" declared Ramsey.

"Secure our families? We ain't got time for that shit nigga, we need to move now" replied Dread.

"Yo Rah" spoke Tommy for the first time since the girls left. "I need to go the movies, and I'm a need to more than once. I can't function right now bro. it can't wait."

"Tommy, I'm wit you my nigga, but we gotta be smart about this. We're dealing with Mexicans, and the mob. We don't even know what cartel these niggas is runnin wit. We can't let emotions cloud our judgment. Besides, they know exactly who we are and they've already threatened our world."

"Threatened our world, nigga what the fuck is you talkin bout" retorted Dread.

"Two mob associates just informed me that I have twenty-four hours to return the money or we're all dead."

"When did this happen?" asked Dread.

"When I was leaving the spital."

"So whadda we do?" Asked Tommy.

"Fuck you mean whadda we do" screamed Dread. "My nigga Deebs is battling for his life behind this bread, niggas ain't givin back shit."

"You ready to risk Tommy's kids behind this shit, my kids behind shit!"

"You sounding like a real bitch right now Rah" replied Tommy dryly.

"Word" inputted Dread. "We're talkin an OG in critical and five million dollars."

"Five million fake dollars."

"Tek di weed and leave di wat" said Dread in a Jamaican accent."

"Yeah man, the passenger was an informant for the feds and they found ten thousand dollars of fake money on Deebs' Inside Man.

"Informant for the feds!" yelled Dread.

"Yeah nigga" yelled back Ramsey "what the fuck, is you listenin" continued Ramsey as he made his checkmate move. "This shit is bigger than just playing cowboy and getting some get back. I got someone on the inside doing some digging. I'm gonna buy us some time to get our families safe and then we gonna deal wit this shit head on."

"We got like eight safe houses dead on the block, not to mention scattered all through the hood" suggested Tommy.

"Nigga is you crazy?" replied Dread

"Actually that just might work" said Ramsey. Dread, get Notty on the phone. Tell him to clear out two houses for now, we'll work on the rest later. Tommy you get all your B.M.s and kids over there and any family you think may be in danger. We got enough soldiers to"

"Nigga is both you niggas fuckin smoking? First off Desirae won't even drive past Franklin Park let alone come back to the block. And how the fuck you gonna get Toya to go along wit this shit. She laid up with that fuckin cracker, she ain't" Dread stopped mid-sentence. He noticed Ramsey had pivoted his right foot back. Tommy noticed it to and stepped in the middle of Ramsey and Dread.

"You want me talk to Toya?" asked Tommy

"No" replied Ramsey as he iced Dread down. "I'll take care of her and Desirae myself. You niggas just get your families safe, I'll get wit you later" finished Ramsey as he exited the apartment.

Chapter 30

Heaven gave the valet a hundred-dollar tip.

"If you do your job correctly, next time maybe you'll get a real Ms. Heaven tip."

The valet couldn't believe he was staring at a single Benjamin Franklin, he secretly cursed himself for talking shit with his coworker instead of paying attention.

"Thank you Ms. Heaven, I promise to do better next time" answered the attendant.

Heaven and Michael pulled off. Michael couldn't lie to himself that orange duck was the best he'd ever had. The experience at the restaurant was one Michael would never forget. Everyone treated Heaven like royalty; the only thing missing was the petals being thrown at her feet as she walked. Heaven chuckled to herself, as she eavesdropped on Michael's thoughts.

"So what would you like to do for a night cap" asked Heaven.

"Nothing really, honestly I'd like to just go back to my hotel and get some sleep".

"Oh don't be a party pooper Michael, let's hit a night club or something. Please, pretty please?"

"Lead the way my queen," sighed Michael. Michael was finding it harder and harder to resist Heaven and he didn't know why. They cruised for about fifteen minutes. Heaven blasted R&B music the whole ride, singing along to each song. Although she was off key, Michael couldn't help but adore her carefree spirit. They pulled up to a club walled by large glass windows. The line for the club reached around the corner and then some, with all types of ethnicities waiting to get in. Heaven pulled in front of the valet and exited the car with Michael following her lead. As she did at the restaurant, Heaven ignored the line and proceeded straight to the front entrance.

"Hey Bruno," said Heaven to the dark haired, 6'9" bouncer. Bruno had muscles in places Michael didn't even know existed.

"What's up Heaven? Who's the new 'boy toy'?"

"Bruno, this is Michael. Michael, Bruno."

Michael and Bruno shook hands while the crowd outside began to get even more restless.

"Rough crowd I see" commented Heaven.

"Pussies" replied Bruno. "Well don't let me hold you love birds up, go inside and enjoy yourselves".

Michael and Heaven walked in, Heaven simply waived at the cashier and walked into the club with Michael. Puff Daddy's *Hello Good Morning* song blared through the speakers as Heaven made her way to the V.I.P. section with Michael close behind. After taking their seats, Heaven flagged down a waitress who seemed to recognize Heaven immediately and scurried off without a word of instruction. Besides Michael and Heaven there was only about twenty other people in the roped off V.I.P. section. Just as fast as she left, the waitress reappeared with two bottles of Dom Perignon in a bucket full of ice with two crystal clear glasses. Heaven placed a black card in the waitress's hand which she swiped through the debit machine on her waist. The waitress handed Heaven her receipt while Heaven handed her three single one hundred dollar bills. The waitress managed to keep her composure as she smiled and said thank you to Heaven for the generous tip.

After a few glasses of champagne Michael started to loosen up, bobbing his head to the music and taking off his blazer.

"It seems you have an admirer," pointed Heaven to a brunette who had been staring at Michael since he and Heaven had entered the V.I.P. section.

Heaven casually beckoned the woman over. At 5'5" and 120 pounds, the brunette proved to be quite stunning. Her olive skin and pointy nose along with a set of voluptuous breasts enabled her to get her desires at all times. The brunette bounced towards Michael and Heaven. Heaven offered the woman a glass of champagne while the brunette openly ogled Michael. The woman sipped the champagne but was still a little nervous about acting on her attraction towards Michael. Heaven leaned back in her seat next to Michael and tousled his hair while the brunette just stood there.

"Well don't be shy" said Heaven. "Entertain the young man!"

As if given the proper cue, the woman downed her drink and carelessly tossed the glass over her shoulder. As Willow Smith's '*Whip Your Hair Back and Forth*' boomed from the speakers, the brunette whipped her hair in a wild, circular manner. She then straddled Michael and gyrated in a way an exotic dancer would do for a wealthy man. While the brunette danced on Michael's lap and licked on his left earlobe, Heaven slid her tongue along the right side of his neck. Licking quickly turned into Michael kissing both women; in turn Heaven kisses the brunette.

Well I guess dealing with this crazy bitch does have its perks.

In between groping and kissing, Michael whispered to the brunette "wanna get out of here?"

"I thought you would never ask," grinned the brunette.

As the trio made their way to the door, a bald headed, slightly over-weight, white male rushed toward them.

"Jesse, where the hell are you going?" said Baldy.

"Don't be a douche Pete" slurred Jesse.

"I'm not being a douche; I just want to make sure you're okay. You don't even know these people".

Before Jesse could reply, Heaven cut her off. As Heaven confidently invaded Pete's space, she interjected "Pete is it?"

"Y-y-yeah," stuttered Pete.

Heaven put her mouth right by Pete's ear, allowing her cool champagne breath to tickle his lobe; meanwhile allowing her perfectly round, c-cup breasts to brush along his chest.

"Well Pete," started Heaven. "As much as I'd like to watch my friend over there fuck the brains out of your little girlfriend while I play with my already wet pussy, I'd much rather watch them with your cock in my mouth" finished Heaven as she ever so lightly licked Pete's ear and rubbed his penis.

Pete almost had an orgasm right on the spot. He didn't know what to do or how to think. It was like all his prayers had come true.

"Would you like to join us Pete?" continued Heaven, rubbing Pete's penis with more intensity.

All Pete could do was shake his head yes. Heaven placed her arm firmly in Pete's pants laying hold onto his manhood.

"My, my," said Heaven in surprise. "The ladies have definitely been missing out".

Heaven turned and made her way to the exit, never releasing Pete from her grasp. As the valet pulled the Ferrari up front, Pete noticed immediately that the car was a coupe with no backseat. Assuming Michael would somehow ride upfront with Jesse Pete stopped with a bewildered look.

"Where am I gonna sit?" questioned Pete.

Heaven slyly replied, "That depends on how bad you want this pussy".

As Heaven opened the trunk, she smiled at the bewildered look on Pete's face. She then took Pete's hand and placed it under her dress allowing Pete to feel just how wet she was. Pete's knees began to shake at the soft touch of Heaven's garden.

"It gets even wetter than that," cooed Heaven.

That's when it happened; Pete came onto Heavens hand. Out of embarrassment, Pete tried to step away, but instinctively Heaven stepped with him. Still not removing her grasp, instead she helped him get the rest out. Without regard for anything, Heaven pulled her hand out of his pants and backed away towards the trunk. Pete, like a trained dog, instantly jumped into the trunk and contorted himself into a human basketball. Heaven then closed the trunk and made her way to the driver's seat. Michael met Heaven at the driver door.

"I'm driving, you two make out or something" exclaimed Michael as he took the keys from Heaven and got into the driver's seat.

Chapter 31

As Michael pulled into the driveway, instead of parking in the garage they'd exited from, Heaven directed Michael to the rear of the house. Jesse was completely naked by the time they'd made it to the mansion. Once securely parked in the rear garage, Heaven opened the trunk and helped Pete out. Pete wobbled a little bit as a result of his legs falling asleep.

"I can't feel my legs" whined Pete.

"I tend to have that effect on men" replied Heaven with a smile.

"Where are we?" questioned Pete as he looked around the dimly lit garage with a single parked black van in the corner.

"I think it's called a garage" giggled Jesse.

"Jess, where the hell are your clothes?"

"I think the better question is why your clothes still are on" responded Heaven as she slipped out of her dress.

Heaven's red and black laced bra and thong not only made Pete's jaw drop, but Michael and Jesse's as well. Heaven's name was the perfect description for her body; A flat stomach with a tiny waist and curves where necessary. Even with the bra, you could tell that her chest didn't need any support. Heavens body had somehow placed a mystical spell on the entire room. As she turned her body away from Pete to face Jesse, it was as if you could feel a slight gust of wind as she twisted her body. Heaven walked towards Jesse and cupped one of Jesse's breasts as she kissed her passionately on the lips. Then Heaven turned her head towards Michael and Pete, "welcome to heaven boys," she teased as she took Jesse by the hand and lead the way through the garage door.

The corridor was lit with a bright red glow that flowed evenly from end to end. Identical doors lined each side of the wall. Michael noticed that although none of the doors were numbered, they each had a light bulb above them. None of the light bulbs were on except for one that they had passed a few doors ago. The green glowing bulb gave off a Christmas tree like effect. Heaven instinctively stopped at a door, turned the knob and swung the door open. The room lit up automatically with a dark red glow, similar to the hallway. Heaven greeted each new entree with a kiss before she locked the door. The room looked like a replica of Heaven's bedroom, but before Michael could take in the scenery, Heaven was all over Pete. Heaven sensually stripped off her thong and bra as she pushed Pete onto the bed.

"Take it off," demanded Heaven.

Pete didn't waste any time kicking off his shoes and disrobing. Michael followed Heaven's cue and placed Jesse on the love seat. Michael kissed Jesse from her neck down to her nipples, making his way to her belly. Jesse moaned as Michael expertly used his tongue, finding his way to her soaking wet love spot. Jesse squeezed and rhythmically rubbed her nipples as Michael slowly licked a place where women only dream of a man finding on their own. Heaven had just finished giving Pete a few licks on his penis as she slowly made her way to mount Pete's manhood.

"Don't you think we should, should use protection?" stumbled Pete.

"Trust me baby," whispered Heaven into Pete's ear as she lay on top of him and slowly slid him inside her inch by inch, collapsing her dripping wet lips around his dick. "You're going to want to feel every part of this".

Heaven slowly rode Pete, her pussy drenched, making Pete feel like he could cum any minute. Michael was still pleasuring Jesse when he heard Heaven in his mind.

There's a knife under the love seat.

The back of the love seat faced the bed Heaven and Pete were on, giving Michael a clear view of Heaven who momentarily had her back to him. Instinctively Heaven turned towards Michael, now mounting Pete with her back to him pressing on his thighs to give her better leverage on her grind. Feeling his manhood grow to a size it had never reached before, Michael stopped pleasuring Jesse with his tongue so he could enter her.

Get the knife first.

Michael searched quickly under the love seat and in no time gripped the handle of the knife. He then entered Jesse with a force she never felt before, causing her to scream out the Lord's name in vain. Michael thrust himself in and out of Jesse which only drove Heaven to ride Pete harder, which in turn made Michael go harder on Jesse. Jesse screamed with pleasure while Pete tried his best to keep his moans from turning into screams.

You ready Michael?

Michael raised his blade high in the air, grasping the weapon with two hands. Heaven slowly rolled a razor blade from her tongue into her hands, and laid back completely onto Pete's chest; her head resting right under his throat. Neither Heaven nor Michael lost one step in their sexual rhythm, keeping their victims in total ecstasy. Heaven sensually used her left hand to caress Pete's throat, causing Pete to arch his throat from the simple pleasure of her touch. The intensity quickly turned up as Heaven squirted all over Pete's dick. The feeling caused Pete to almost erupt inside of Heaven.

Now Michael

Michael immediately plunged his knife into Jesse's belly, causing him to cum on impact. At first Jesse didn't know what hit her, her eyes opened as Michael pulled out the knife to raise it for a second plunge. Just as Michael was taking his first stab at Jesse, Heaven placed the blade on the left side of Pete's neck and deeply slit his throat, severing all vocal cords. Heaven then dropped the blade and started slamming her pussy up and down on Pete's dick, causing him to explode inside of Heaven while he grabbed for his jugular. Michael continued to stab

Jesse while he pumped his dick in and out of her until Jesse's eyes were lifeless. Heaven slowed down her slamming to a gentle grind, riding Pete's dick until all the blood drained from the muscle causing Pete's dick to go limp. Heaven then leaned back as she did before, allowing the blood to spread through her hair and drip down her neck. As she bathed in blood Heaven rolled onto her belly while still atop Pete. Relishing in her release Heaven scooted herself up until she was face to face with Pete and kissed him softly on the lips.

Heaven and Michael stared at each other, lost in a world of joy, heat, lust, and euphoria. Heaven stood up and squeezed Pete's semen out of her vagina. Michael watched as the substance dripped down her leg. Michael didn't even realize he was still inside Jesse until he felt his dick become solid granite at his desire for Heaven. Michael yanked himself from Jesse as he threw the bloody knife on the floor, and then stormed towards Heaven.

Yes Michael, come fuck me.

Michael reached for Heaven and backhanded her in the face with all his might, causing Heaven to do a full 180 degree turn. He then grabbed Heaven by her hair and threw her onto the bed face first. Heaven landed on Pete's bloody body, her face sliding all through his warm, red blood. Michael wasted no time as he mounted Heaven from behind and fucked her like a bitch.

"Oh shit, fuck me Michael, yes, fuck me Michael!" screamed Heaven as she produced orgasm after orgasm.

THE GATEWAY

Chapter 32

"No Ram! I'm not packing up the kids and moving on nobody's Esmond Street!" said Toya.

"It's only for a couple of days, just gotta get some things sorted out." Ramsey stood on the porch arguing with his ex-wife in the middle of the night while his sons slept upstairs.

"Sort what out Ram? You won't even tell me what the fuck is going on."

"Look, the less you know, the better."

"Are we in danger Ram? That shit on the news with Deebs, are you involved?"

"Everything okay out here?" asked a white male in his pajamas who just stepped out of the house.

"Yeah Steve," said Toya. "Everything's fine."

"Hey Ramsey."

"What up Steve."

"Is Deebs okay?"

"He's fine Steve."

"That's good, because the news..."

Ramsey cut Steve off, "Look Steve, I'm trying to talk to Toya, so if you don't mind?"

"Don't cut him off like that," interrupted Toya.

"It's okay hun, Ramsey doesn't mean anything by it. He's been through hell today. Can I get you anything Ramsey?"

"No Steve, I just need to talk to Toya."

"Okay, I'll be inside if you guys need anything."

"Great guy Toya," Ram said.

"Fuck you Ram! At least he's here!"

"Look, I don't wanna argue. I just want you and the kids safe."

Toya thought about it for a minute. As much as she'd hate to admit it, she knew Ramsey wouldn't be asking her to do this if it wasn't necessary.

"How long Ramsey?"

"A couple of days."

"How long Ramsey?"

"One week, gimmie a week."

"One week Ramsey and Steve comes too."

"He's not in danger, there's no need for him to come."

"So what, I'm supposed to go without dick for a week because of some shit you did? I don't think so. He's coming."

"What about Steve? Do you think he's going to be comfortable living in the hood?"

"Don't worry; the white boy will be alright."

"Whatever Toya, just be packed and ready by the morning."

"Goodnight Ram," finished Toya as she stepped inside the house and closed the door.

Ramsey walked off the porch to his car. Toya was the easy part. Now Ramsey had to convince Desirae to move on Esmond Street. Ramsey made the slow drive to Desirae's house thinking about the past 24 hours. He was so lost, never before had he ever been in such an out of control situation. How the fuck was he gonna explain why him and three off duty officers were riding with so much fire power, or why he and Deebs even pulled over the Benz. Ramsey couldn't come up with anything that would make sense to IAD, or the Feds. He would have no choice but to lawyer up and say nothing, knowing his silence would be a sign of guilt in itself. What about the Inferno case? He could feel it about to crack and now he was probably off the case. Ramsey didn't even realize he was at Desirae's house until he was pulling into the driveway, staring at Desirae on the porch.

Chapter 33

Desirae sat on the porch with a cup in her hand. Ramsey could smell the alcohol as soon as he reached the porch.

"Hey Ramsey," said Desirae.

"Hey Dez."

"Wanna drink?"

"Sure."

Ramsey watched as Desirae pulled a cup from one of the porch columns, filled to the brim with white liquor.

"He's not going to come out of it Ram," said a concerned Desirae.

"Don't say that Dez, Deebs is the strongest muthafucka I know. Anyone else would have died on the scene," Ramsey replied.

"Why are you here Ram," questioned Desirae.

Ramsey just didn't know how to ask Desirae; Esmond Street was a place of sorrow for her. Her father had been murdered on that street when she was a little girl right in front of her face. Deebs pulled her away from the scene and from then on never left her side until he was forced to by her mother. The day after her father died Desirae left Esmond Street, intending never to return Deebs was the only one Desirae managed to remain in touch with until they got older. Ramsey thought about putting her in a hotel somewhere but that would place whoever he had watching her at risk. Ramsey quickly dismissed moving her out of state; she'd never leave while Deebs was in the hospital.

"I need you to move on Esmond Street for a few days Dez," Ramsey blurted out. Desirae looked up at Ramsey, cocked her head to the side for a minute and finally just glared at him. She then rolled her head back and guzzled her drink until the cup was empty.

"I'm going to go to bed Ramsey," slurred Desirae as she tried to get up; although as quickly as she got up, she stumbled and fell into Ramsey's arms. Tears filled Desirae's eyes as she began to sob, paining for Deebs to come back to her. Ramsey carried Desirae to his car and placed her in the backseat. Desirae wasn't just in danger from The Mob; she was in danger from herself. Guilt began to solidify around the outskirts of Ramsey's heart. He fought back the tears as he drove towards Boston. Ramsey couldn't choke up now; he couldn't let guilt smother his judgment. This was the price of being a leader; he had to put his emotions and well-being to the side while he cared for the well-being of others. Ramsey was drained, he knew he had a lot to think about but he needed rest to think clearly. Once he reached Esmond Street Ramsey carried Desirae into the safe house and laid her down on the bed. Ramsey didn't want Desirae waking up and freaking out, or even waking up and sneaking out, so he placed a chair in front of the door and took a seat. Finally, for the first time in what seemed like forever, Ramsey let his problems float away, closed his eyes and slept.

Chapter 34

Ramsey woke up before Desirae did. The room he had for Desirae had its own shower and bathroom in it. He looked at Desirae and figured she'd be asleep for another hour or so. Before knocking out, Ramsey had sent someone to Desirae's house to pick up some clothes and make sure the house was secured. The drawers and closets of the safe houses they kept stayed filled with a variety of men and women's clothing; So Ramsey simply grabbed a pair of boxers, a t-shirt, and a pair of jeans before he made his way to the shower. The bathroom was basic but quaint, with powder blue curtains to match the blue tiles and blue wallpaper. The sink, toilet, and tub were porcelain white, that were cleaned everyday by neighborhood kids for a small fee.

The water hit Ramsey hard, gradually going from cold to warm then to a nice steamy hot. The first shock of cold water woke Ramsey up completely. His senses surged alive, his brain was spinning at full speed while his mind felt as sharp as ever. He'd decided to tell Desirae the truth; it was the only way he was going to be able to convince her to remain at the safe house. It wasn't like Deebs didn't tell his wife everything anyways. Desirae was Deebs' best friend; with no children they spent more time together than any other couple Ramsey knew. Ramsey already felt responsible for Deebs' condition, and the task of explaining what happened to Desirae was making feelings of trepidation wave over him. God willing, Deebs was going to fully recover, and Ramsey couldn't imagine having to explain to Deebs that Desirae was killed behind the same thing that got Deebs shot. Ramsey pondered on how he would deal with the counterfeit money and what the ramifications of returning the money would produce. Although Ramsey wasn't sure how deep the Feds had infiltrated The Mob, or the Columbians for that matter; if he could simply return the money and walk away without consequence, he would. Were the Feds only after the money? Did they have other informants? Whose fake money was it, The Mob or the Feds? These were all questions Ramsey needed the answers to.

Ramsey quickly finished up his shower; he had a lot to do and not much time to do it. Ramsey dressed himself in the bathroom, the pants were a little big for him but all in all he looked good. Ramsey walked out of the bathroom to see Desirae putting on her shoes.

"Morning Dez," said Ramsey.

"Don't 'morning Dez' me Ram. Why the fuck am I here? Better yet, how the fuck did I get here?" Desirae was steaming and Ramsey knew it.

"Just sit down for a second and let me explain."

"I don't wanna hear it Ramsey, I'm going to see Deebs, and when he gets better- I'm a make sure he fucks you up for bringing me to this fucking street," yelled Desirae as she looked for a purse she didn't have.

"Where the fuck is my purse!" screamed Desirae aloud.

"Desirae your life is in danger," exclaimed Ramsey, "And so is Deebs' if you don't stay here." Desirae glared at Ramsey with fire in her eyes.

"Why am I in danger Ramsey?"
"The people who shot Deebs are after us and our families."
"Why?"
"Look Dez, the less you know the better. You can invoke spousal privilege for Deebs but not for me, Tommy, and Dread. Please you have to trust me."
"What about Deebs? How am I supposed to see him and who's watching him?"   "You'll have an escort take you back and forth to see Deebs and there'll be guards on Deebs' side 24 hours a day, but I need you to cooperate with me and your escorts Desirae… It's the only way I can minimize the danger you're in."

Desirae dropped onto the bed. Tears attacked her as she placed her face in her hands and sobbed. Desirae's world was crashing, she felt as if she'd already lost Deebs, just as she lost her father. Sadness, fear, and misery invaded her heart all at once. The thought of living without Deebs formed a cloud of depression around her very soul.

Ramsey sat next to Desirae and hugged her tightly. He wanted to promise her that everything would be alright. That Deebs would recover and no harm would come to any of them, but he couldn't. So he simply held Desirae until she cried herself into exhaustion. Ramsey told Desirae that whenever she was ready to see Deebs that all she had to do was notify the guard at the door and that she had clothes hanging in the closet from her home. Ramsey kissed her forehead, tucked her back into bed, and promised to return.

Chapter 35

Ramsey drove with a newfound determination. He swore that he would die or worse, go to prison, before he let any harm come to Desirae. Ramsey pulled out his phone and called Toya.

"I'm sending someone to pick you guys up," said Ramsey. "Why aren't you coming to get us?"
"I have shit to do Toya, just do as I tell you and please don't give the people I have watching you a hard time."

"Fuck you Ramsey. I didn't get myself or the boys into this shit, you did! So don't act like you're doing me any fuckin' favors."
"So how the fuck do you want me to act when you're giving me such a hard time about this shit?"

"Act like you're not fucking inconveniencing me."
"Look Toya, I'm sorry that I've placed you in this situation, and as much as it's my fault I need you to pretend that it's yours so I can rectify this situation without anyone getting hurt. Can you do that Toya? If not for me, can you do it for our sons?"

Toya merely hung up the phone. Ramsey knew that meant okay. Ramsey hated what the Inferno case did to his marriage; they used to be so happy. Ramsey had once loved, admired, even envied Toya's fire, now it just made him miserable at times. Ramsey placed another call before he got caught up in thinking about Toya.

"Tommy, everything good on your end?"

"Yeah Ram, I got all these unstable creatures in the van now with the kids... how 'bout you?"

"Dez is already there and someone's going to get Toya now."

"I told you nigga!" yelled Tommy to Dread.

"I want my dolla as soon as you get change nigga! What you doin' now Ram?"

"I'm headed to the precinct."

"Whaddaya gonna say?"

"Nothing, I don't know enough to try and fix this shit. I'm a give a call to a friend in the hen house and see what I can find out about this informant."

"Damn nigga, I was hoping you'd come up with somethin' by now, fuck it though. You gonna visit Deebs today?"

"Yeah, probably later. Yo, see about getting a few SWAT niggas to watch Deebs around the clock."

"Yeah, I already got that done. Anything else?"

"Naw, just stay on point and keep Dread out of trouble."

"No doubt, holla at me my nig!"

"One."

"One."

Chapter 36

Ramsey pulled up to the precinct and parked in the back. Officers acknowledged Ramsey and gave their best wishes in hopes for Deebs' recovery. Ramsey accepted the sympathy with a simple nod. Ramsey noticed Berta by her desk and made his way over to her. "So what's the word Berrr-Breezy?" asked Ramsey as he sat atop Berta's desk.

"Nothing much, how's Deebs doing?"
"I haven't been by to see him yet today." Ramsey looked around the precinct with a weary look.

"The Feds are in Furnari's office."

"Yeah, I figured that. So what happened with your triple case?""Better than I expected. He still had the murder weapon when we executed the warrant. These guys never cease to amaze me. I mean a couple of episodes of *First 48* and you should know a few no-noes."Ramsey chuckled as he watched Furnari's door open while two agents exited the office. Furnari stood in the threshold of his office as he beckoned Ramsey over.

"Here we go," sighed Ramsey as he slid off Berta's desk.

"Good luck Ram," Berta replied. Ramsey smiled at Berta and made his way over to Furnari's office. Furnari sternly closed the door behind Ramsey, just as Ramsey noticed two agents sitting at Furnari's desk.

"Detective Ramsey," started Furnari, "this is agent Rosenberg and Lehman."

Ramsey laughed to himself as he thought, 'two Jews on a money case… I'm through'.

"Is there something funny detective," questioned Lehman. Lehman's long blonde hair was pulled back into a ponytail. Her icy blue eyes reminded Ramsey of icebergs breaking and falling into ocean water. Her look was plain. She was short, a little pudgy, no real waist, with an average size chest; but her eyes were absolutely captivating.

"The lady asked you a question," interjected Rosenberg. His dark brown hair with eyes to match flowed well with his square jaw. Rosenberg had square shoulders and stood at over six feet tall with a fit physique. His voice was deep and sort of boomed at Ramsey. With Rosenberg's voice and Lehman's eyes, they made for a very intimidating interrogation team. Ramsey had no plans of talking, he wanted to extract whatever information he could from these agents. Ramsey knew he would have to be extremely careful. "I'm sorry," smiled Ramsey. "I was just captivated by Lehman's icy blues".

Agent Lehman stepped closer to Ramsey leaving very little space in between them.

"I assure you detective; my eyes should be the last thing that captivates you. Care to find a place where we can talk?"

"I'd be honored," smiled Ramsey. Ramsey led the way to the interrogation room located down the hall. All the room contained was four chairs and a black table with silver legs outside of the standard camera and two way mirrors. Furnari didn't bother entering the room and watched through the mirror. Ramsey took a seat and watched as Lehman took a seat across from him while Rosenberg remained standing with his arms crossed.

"So detective," began Lehman. "Tell us what exactly you, Deebs, and two members of the SWAT team were doing making an off duty car stop".

"What, no cigarette and soda?" grinned Ramsey.

"Just answer the fucking question detective," snapped Rosenberg without moving an inch.

Ramsey just looked at the agents. "Okay," said Lehman, "how about you tell us who fired first? Was it the car full of Mexicans, you...Deebs?"

Still Ramsey said nothing.

"Look detective, it's no mystery that you were there. Keeping your badge is just about impossible, but if you talk to us, maybe we can keep you out of prison," said Lehman.

At that moment, the story came to Ramsey. He knew not to say anything but a scenario that would save him, Deebs, Tommy, and Dread, and that's exactly what came to him. All Ramsey needed now was access to the witness statements.

"I have a question," said Ramsey.

"What you should have is answers," boomed Rosenberg.

"And what you should have is better manners" retorted Ramsey with a glare.

"What's your question detective?" asked Lehman.

"Why are the Feds involved in this? I mean at worst, this is a case of a questionable stop gone badly. What would the Feds have to do with this?"

"The passenger in the Benz was a federal informant detective. He was very instrumental to an ongoing investigation and we are very much interested in why he died," answered Lehman.

"If he was so important, why weren't you guys keeping closer tabs on him?""Oh but we did have close tabs on him detective," slyly smiled Lehman.

"Why weren't the locals informed?" retorted Ramsey.

"Cause it was none of your fucking business," yelled Rosenberg, who was obviously growing tired of Ramsey and Lehman's cat and mouse game.

"I don't think your partner likes me," whispered Ramsey in Lehman's direction."I don't think he does either, but to answer your question with a question, why should the Feds inform the locals about a federal investigation?"

"Because there's a possibility that the locals are running a parallel investigation with another informant involved in the same investigation the Feds are running."

"Is that what happened detective? You were running an investigation involving one of the victims?" asked Lehman.

"All I'm doing is answering your question as to why there should be open communication between federal and local police," responded Ramsey.

Rosenberg suddenly slammed his hands loudly on the table yelling, "Where's the fucking money detective?"

"You know momma always use to say people who continuously curse demonstrate a lack of vocabulary," replied Ramsey as he sat back.

Lehman couldn't help but laugh.

"I want my rep," stated Ramsey.

Ten seconds later Furnari burst into the interrogation room. "Interview's over," exclaimed Furnari. Rosenberg stormed out while Lehman slowly rose to her feet. "Thank you for your time detective.

Like we told both detective Jackson and detective Johnson, I look forward to making your acquaintance. I'll be seeing you soon detective," finished Lehman as she started her walk out of the room.

"Make sure you leave your partner at home," called Ramsey after her.

"In my office detective!" said Furnari as he walked out.Ramsey pondered how he handled the interview. He wondered if he lawyered up too early or too late. Could he have gotten more information? Now he had to think about what his next moves were going to be. Ramsey walked into Furnari's office and instinctively took his gun off of his waist, unclipped his badge and placed them on Furnari's desk.

"What're you doing!" exclaimed Furnari.

"Saving you the breath of telling me I'm suspended until further notice," answered Ramsey.

"Sit down Ramsey," ordered Furnari. Ramsey did as he was told. "Look Detective, I don't know what kind of shit you got yourself into and personally, I don't care. What I do know is that I want this Inferno case solved and I don't have anyone better than you for the job. If you're going to federal prison, you make sure you got this Inferno case solved first. Now get the fuck out of my office."

A little confused, Ramsey picked up his gun and badge and walked out of Furnari's office without a word.

Ramsey walked to his desk and checked his messages. He had a few miscellaneous messages and some messages from Kinkay. Ramsey dialed Kinkay up.

"Hello?" answered Kinkay.

"Hey love," replied Ramsey."What the fuck Ramsey! You don't know how to return someone's call?""Sorry babe, I've been under the gun.""Whatever Ram, just get your ass down here before I trash this treasure trove of information."

"On my way!" Ramsey quickly hung up the phone and made his way to Kinkay's office.

Chapter 37

Michael sat at the table with Heaven, Matt, and Marr. Suela made an elaborate breakfast for them. Michael recognized the China pattern, it was a First Period Worcester Porcelain in the Phoenix Pattern., The food was brought out in waves, but in small portions so Michael would try everything. Suela paraded popular and not so popular breakfast dishes from all over the world back and forth to the dining table. As everyone ate Suela would give a rundown on the history of the food they were currently dining on. It was as if with each new taste Michael was transported to another country. As Suela spoke and the picture came into focus. With every chew the culture and area that Suela described became more vivid. Pretty soon Michael felt like he was on an endless rollercoaster through time, as scenes and people around him constantly changed as he sat, ate, and watched.

Michael spent the previous day riding around Santa Monica with Heaven. They shopped, had lunch, dinner and caught a late night movie. They didn't do much talking during the course of their day, instead they observed each other; learning about each person through their interactions with other people. To Michael, Heaven was a bit of a snob. She was very demanding and spoke her mind regardless of how she made people feel. She also had a way of turning people into putty in her hand. At first Michael thought it was just her looks, but he slowly started to realize that Heaven possessed some type of energy that made others helpless around her. Heaven was really beginning to enjoy Michael. He was smart, polite, gentle and very attentive to a woman's sexual needs. She greatly appreciated Michael's attention to detail, like how even at a glance he noticed the change of blush she was using or how she did her eyebrows. Not to mention the fact that he was gorgeous. Heaven in her own persuasive way convinced Michael not to go through with his plastic surgery. She told him it would've been a sin to destroy such a craftsmanship of God, like his face.

As much as Heaven adored Michael, she felt he was wasting his inner-being. Heaven thought of Seduce as a gift from God, and now she had an opportunity through Michael to make her breed line stronger.

Michael was sipping his coffee quietly, trying his best not to think, afraid that everyone would be reading his mind.

"So Michael," started Matt, "what made you pick up and leave good ole' Massachusetts?" "Just wanted a fresh start," responded Michael. "And of all the states to fly into, you had to fly into mine?" mimicked Marr, doing a pretty good Casanova impression.

"I had my reasons," replied Michael.

"So when can we take a field trip too good ole' Mass?" questioned Matt. "I can't go back," said Michael as he dropped his head with thoughts of Candace and his two boys. Heaven gave Michael a slight glare when Michael wasn't looking.

So pathetic.

Matt and Marr instinctively looked at Heaven.

"Why not?" pried Marr.

Not wanting to give them any of the facts but wanting to sound believable as well, Michael gave them what they wanted.

"I have a warrant out for my arrest," Michael admitted.

"A warrant?" said Matt. "Why, what in the world for?" continued Marr.

"Murder, and I have the best cop in the state working the case, a detective named Ramsey" answered Michael.

Matt and Marr caught eyes; they simply loved the idea of a good old fashion detective case. Good versus evil, mano y mano or in their case mano y manos.

"Tell us more of this Detective Ramsey," inquired Matt.

"Well there's really not much to say. He's as smart as a whip; FBI/CIA material. He's closed just about every case that's come across his desk and his obsession with my case in unnerving."

"What else?" asked Marr, perking up in his seat.

Heaven could see where the conversation was going and decided to excuse herself from the table. She and Michael didn't get in until five in the morning, and she'd only gotten about a half hour of sleep before Matt and Marr practically dragged them out of bed for breakfast.

"I'm going to bed Michael, if you like you can join me when you're done," replied Heaven. "So what else?" jumped in Matt before Michael could escape. "What else like what?" asked Michael. "Is he married, kids, hobbies, you know; things like that," stated Marr.

"He's divorced with two boys, he's close to the forensic officer also working my case and he's sleeping with some prostitute from Georgia," answered Michael.

"Well someone's done their homework," said Marr

"Excuse you sir, foul ball. That was my line. Is he a loner cop" asked Matt as he scowled at Marr.

"Yes and no, he's a homicide detective and he works alone but he has three other cop friends and they're tight as thieves," said Michael.

Michael knew about Kinkay and Cherry from his long nights watching and studying Ramsey. He also knew about Ramsey's hideout, along with Ramsey's little crew. Although Michael never saw Ramsey do anything illegal, Michael was positive that Ramsey was dirty. How else did Ramsey think like a criminal well enough to catch them?

Matt and Marr were taking mental notes of everything Michael said. Matt had a savant like memory, enabling him to retain 98% of anything he heard, read, or saw.

"Is there anything else you can tell us about this Ramsey?" continued Marr. "Look guys," said Michael rising to his feet. "I'm fucking beat, I'm struggling just to keep my eyes open, can we finish this later?"

"Our apologies" began Matt.

"Yes, yes we're quite sorry, please go ahead and rest," ended Marr.

"Don't worry about the dishes."

"No don't worry, Suela will get them". Michael got up and made his way out of the kitchen.

"Are you thinking what I'm thinking?"

"Well it's the middle of spring," answered Marr.

"And Boston is lovely this time of year."

"And we've never played a cross country game."

"And this Ramsey fellow sounds absolutely yummy."

"Yes, it's been a long time since we've had a good fox hunt."

"Indeed. All the hunters out here have either been out foxed or out hunted."

"Then it's settled."

"I would say so."

"Suela!" yelled Matt. "Pack the peanuts and our best bottle of Napa Valley!" finished Marr as he grinned at Matt. "The M-N-M Killers" were on their way to Massachusetts.

Chapter 38

At first Michael thought it was because he was tired why he was so disoriented and finding it difficult to remember how to get to Heaven's room. Michael was usually much better with his sense of direction. He'd been back and forth to Heaven's room enough to remember how to get there with his eyes closed. Michael realized what was happening by the time he reached Heaven's door. For the first time he was begging for her to intrude into his mind and give out directions. Michael heard Suela down the hall and called out to her. After getting the directions, Michael made his way to Heaven's room. As Michael reached for the door The Voice talked to him for the first time in what seemed like forever.

SLOWLY MICHAEL, TRY NOT TO WAKE HER.

What Michael recognized more than anything else was the disorientated feeling he'd had before touching the door. Whenever Michael had that feeling he would lose big chunks of time, not being able to recall anything after the disorientated feeling. Michael was sure whatever happened during the blackout involved murdering someone, he'd woken from too many blackouts covered in blood. Michael slowly and carefully opened the door, the deep plush crimson red carpet muffled Michael's feet and whatever sounds they would've made. The Voice had to make sure Heaven was asleep so he could talk to Michael freely. Michael silently made his way across the room and into the private bathroom.

SIT DOWN IN THE CHAIR MICHAEL, WE NEED TO TALK. Michael did as he was told and sat down in the chair.

YOU NEED TO KILL THEM MICHAEL. TONIGHT. ALL OF THEM. No Mikey don't she's like us, they're like us, we're home Mikey. We're home.

Michael was taken back a bit, The Voice never said one thing and then went against it.

MICHAEL THIS IS A DANGEROUS SITUATION YOU'RE IN. KILL THEM AND LEAVE!

Michael's head was all jumbled inside his thought process was knocked off its axis.

You don't have to kill her Mikey; we could just stay here. All day we can kill, party, have sex, it'll be a blast.

REMEMBER THE MISSION MICHAEL.

"And exactly what is the mission?" said Michael out loud just as Heaven entered the bathroom.

"Come to bed Michael, let me make it better."

Chapter 39

It had been twenty-three hours since Ramsey had gotten out of the car with the mobsters. Things were moving according to schedule, but Ramsey could tell Dread, Tommy, and the rest of Monster Squad were running out of patience. Ramsey hadn't told anyone but the problem had become even more complicated. The mob's reach was long enough to make the Deebs investigation go away for Ramsey and his team. Special Ringtone called it a bonus. Ramsey's phone rang.

"What up?"

"Yo Ram where you at?" asked Dread.

"Headed to you and Tommy now, ya'll ready to roll?"

"Yeah we good, let's shake and bake on these niggas."

"Be there in a sec."

Tommy and Dread had found a fence for the money. They could get thirty dollars on every hundred. The suggestion to take the money and use it to fund the war against the mob sounded appealing to someone bent on revenge. But Ramsey liked the idea of being a free man a little better. The money was in Dread's possession, Ramsey hoped all he was going to have to do was lie to get it from him.

Ramsey pulled up to the spot only to see a fresh new trick or treat van parked out front. 'Fuck' is all Ramsey could think to himself. Ramsey entered the spot to see Dread, Tommy, Sinn, Putt, Notty, Swagg-G, and a few other soldiers all geared up in S.W.A.T. wear and street clothes.

"What the fuck is this?" questioned Ramsey.

"Since we know we're supposed to be meeting these muthafuckas in less than an hour we might as well send a loud and clear message" offered Dread.

"And whose idea was this?"

"Mines" spoke Tommy. "It's unexpected, strategic, and smart. We're doing this."

"Are you niggas…" Ramsey's phone cut him off, it was Kinkay's ringtone. Ramsey quickly hit the ignore button. "A yo, ya'll niggas roll out front for a minute. Let me holla at these niggas."

Notty looked at Dread. Dread stared Ramsey down for a good thirty seconds before he turned to Notty and gave the head nod for them to leave.

Just as they were closing the door, Ramsey's phone went off again. It was Kinkay. Ramsey ignored it.

"We need to think about this ya'll" started Ramsey. "I know emotions are high." Kinkay's ringtone cut Ramsey off again. He ignored it. "Fuck man."

"Fuck man what!" blurted Dread. "Why the fuck you tryin to stop us. And who the fuck keep callin you Ram? What the fuck nigga, what type a time is you on."

Before Ramsey could respond Kinkay's ringtone went off again.

"Answer it," said Tommy.

"Kinkay, not right now," answered Ramsey.

"Put it on speaker phone," ordered Dread.

"Guess again my friend," came through the phone as Ramsey put it on speaker.

"Hello. Who is this?" replied Ramsey as he hit the record button on his phone.

"Why we're your new play mates Detective," said another voice.

"Oh where going to have so much fun," cheered the first voice.

"Now the rules are quite simple Detective," said the second voice.

"Such lovely geraniums," bellowed the first voice.

Suddenly female screams of excruciating pain blared through the phone. The screams continued for what seemed like hours. Finally, the screaming stopped, it was apparent she'd passed out from the shock.

"Now that was awfully rude," scolded the second voice

"Oh, don't be a wanker," whined the first voice

"Tick."

"What?" replied Ramsey.

"Tock."

"Wait."

"Tick."

"What're the rules?"

"Tock."

Chapter 40

"What the fuck was that?" asked a bewildered Dread.

"I gotta go fellas. Look I got no time explain or try to reason with you guys. The mob has a contact that can make the whole Deebs and cartel investigation go away. Giving the money back, getting this case off our shoulders, and dealing with the mob on a later note is our best move."

"Fuck" started Dread but Ramsey cut him off.

"Fuck nothing, this is straight form the top, Special Ringtone ordered. We give the money back, and we move later. It's done. Here's the address to the drop. Don't fuck around nigga," finished Ramsey as he handed Dread the address on a piece of paper and high tailed it out of the apartment.

No one said anything to Ramsey as he rushed passed, jumped in his unmarked car and threw on the lights. Ramsey's mind was spinning with thoughts. 'Someone had taken Kinkay, but why?' Ramsey grabbed his car radio.

"This is detective Ramsey. I need all units at 56 Milton Avenue now. Officer down, all units respond."

Ramsey weaved through traffic as if the spirit of Swagg-G had entered his body. Ramsey arrived at the scene just as two blue and white officers started to ascend the porch.

"Officers" yelled Ramsey. "Hold up, I called it in, I'm taking lead on this one."

Ramsey walked into the house with his gun drawn. He'd noticed from outside that all the lights in the home appeared to be on. As the three men entered the home one look to the left ended all needs for a search. Blood adorned Kinkay's living room in an indescribable and horrific manner. In the middle of the floor laid Kinkay's shiatsu. The dog had been sliced open from the top of his stomach line to the bottom.

"Nobody move, nobody touch anything," Ramsey spoke clear and controlled. Ramsey quickly removed his shoes and a pair of footsies from his back pocket. After placing on his footsies Ramsey entered the crime scene. The blood pattern explained a lot about the killer. Ramsey's first thought was that this was not Inferno. The scene seemed staged and wild at the same time, the Inferno killings were a little more methodical with less emotion. This killing seemed planned because of the way the dog was laid out but the scene seemed more violent than it should be. Blood was everywhere, from the floor to the ceiling and yet there was no human body. Ramsey took a closer at the dog. The inside of the dog's stomach seemed to have something inside of it. As Ramsey looked closer, he saw one thing that surprised him and another that frightened him. Within the dog laid a bright red cherry and a small torn badge made of cotton. To the right of the dog Ramsey could see a half filled bottle of Screaming Eagle Cabernet Sauvignon and a champagne glass. At the time this seemed irrelevant to Ramsey, but he stored the item in his mental file cabinet anyway. No clue could be ignored at this point, the caller's words stung inside Ramsey's mind.

Ramsey flew with lighting speed past the officers and out the door to his car. In one single motion Ramsey was flying back into Boston, this time his lights were off. Ramsey's mind was in full swing, nothing was taking long to deduce, the clues were too obvious, and Kinkay's life depended solely on his reaction time. The cherry was clear where Ramsey was to head next, but the badge was the monkey wrench. The badge was from his first years joining the SEALs. The class he came up with had created the badge as a symbol of going dark. Ramsey was to have no police assistance on this one, it was him versus the kidnappers.

Chapter 41

Michael and Heaven walked the grass fields that covered four acres behind the massive mansion. For years Michael had felt like Candace was the only woman he could ever love. But when it came time to kill her, Michael had done it. His hesitancy to kill Heaven when instructed had been plaguing him. It was something about Heaven that made Michael feel whole.

"So Michael, what're you going to do when you leave here?" asked Heaven.

"I don't know; I guess I'll figure it out as I go along."

"So why did you come here in the first place?"

"I don't know, my… The Voice told me to come here."

"Is The Voice not talking to you anymore?"

"Yes, but not like before I met you."

Michael's relationship with his voice concerned Heaven and Seduce. But Michael was so gorgeous, not to mention the way he handled himself in their recent sex-kill-a-thon, made Heaven feel alive for the first time again in decades. Michael reminded Heaven of Tibias. Tibias was the only man Heaven had ever loved, dating back to her childhood in the insignificant town of Burns Kansas. Heaven always loved Tibias, she loved him before she had Seduce and continued to love Tibias after Seduce. Despite all the awful things that happened to her growing up Heaven still managed to find love in the eyes of a sweet and caring young man. Losing Tibias had almost driven Heaven to suicide. Thinking about her wounded past caused Heaven to tear up.

"Well I'm going to hate seeing you leave," said Heaven as she wiped her eyes.

"Don't cry, why don't you come with me?" offered Michael

"And live off what, your good looks?" smiled Heaven. "And they are good" said Heaven as she slightly cupped Michael's face.

"I just don't wanna lose you, not now at least" replied Michael.

Still touching his face "you'll never lose me Michael, we share a bond that will transcend space and time. But we'll talk about that later. I received a message from Matt and Marr earlier. They're bringing a guest home for dinner, which is always a special occasion. I never let Suela prepare when they bring a guest home, would you mind helping me prepare, it may take a few hours.

"I hope it takes an eternity" answered Michael as he kissed Heaven softly on the lips.

"You really know how to sweep a girl off her feet huh?" whispered Heaven into Michael's ear after drawing away from his lips.

"You could have fooled me" whispered Michael back. "I'm the one that's convinced he's flying right now."

THE GATEWAY

Chapter 42

Ramsey entered Cherry's house from the back door, using a spare key he'd made. Ramsey never used the key before, but he kept it in case of an emergency. Cherry's house was completely dark and silent. Instead of turning the lights on, Ramsey's eyes adjusted as if he were part owl. Ramsey didn't mind the dark, it's where he did his best work.

Based on what he just experienced at Kinkay's home, Ramsey didn't expect the killers to be discrete for very long, just long enough for him to get a head start on the police. Ramsey found Cherry laying in the living room. Her ankles and wrist were sawed off by a rusty hacksaw that lay covered in blood on the floor. Ramsey played the recorded conversation on his phone between him and Kinkay's abductors. The screams through the phone resonated in Ramsey's head. The pitch of the scream became clear, the tone accurate. It was Cherry that Tommy, Dread, and he had listen to scream in agony.

Ramsey refocused on the crime scene again, immediately he saw three things that stood out of place like a series of pictures that his son's teacher would send home on a piece of paper for his son to figure which picture didn't belong. The L.A. badge was an easy read, but the two green peanut M&Ms made no sense to Ramsey whatsoever. Cherry's body was still fresh. Ramsey touched the blood only to find that it was still warm. Too warm for the killers to kill Cherry, kidnap

Kinkay and then call him. The scene replayed in Ramsey's head again, this time with slight variations. The picture was now split like a dual monitor. On one screen Ramsey could see Kinkay being attacked. In Ramsey's mind the man attacking Kinkay was big and savage. Ramsey could see the anger and violence vibrating from the beast. The manner in which he killed the dog allowed Ramsey to peer into the man's soul. At the same time on the other screen Ramsey saw a totally different man. The man was small, and frail. He looked weak, but his eyes burned with a strong intensity. Ramsey cringed at the images of the man methodically taking his time to cut through Cherry's body. It wasn't the act that made Ramsey cringe, it was the way in which the man performed it. The man was so relaxed, Ramsey could see him talking to Cherry calmly as she screamed in pain. His detachment from the situation made Ramsey put this man in a category way beyond any level of psycho he would put Inferno in. Ramsey pictured Cherry putting up a good fight because of her size and athleticism but the man was also smart, and outwitted Cherry to her own demise.

Ramsey exited Cherry's home, the air hit his nostrils. Ramsey inhaled deeply, he was trying to clear emotion from his thought process. Graphic images of Cherry randomly collided against Ramsey's skull as he tried to string together something, anything. For some reason the M&M's kept coming back to Ramsey's mind, it was something one of his go to tech guys had said about killer M&M's.

"Raaminator, where the fuck you been bud?" said the person Ramsey called.

"Geeker, this is not a social call. I need you working now bro."

"Right. Sorry about that. I was out of the country, no real tools to do what you wanted. The Sloan thing right, I'm all over it."

"Later for that Geeker, we got some other shit that needs our attention like now."

"Whadda ya need Ram?"

"What do you know about murders involving M&Ms."

"Did you say M&Ms?"

"Yeah I know it sounds crazy but."

"No, no, man two M&Ms, if it's not a copycat then it's connected to these string of murders that's been happening all over the world. People call them the M&M killers, kind of cheesy, but anyway, these guys are supposed to be fucking sick, I mean like retard sick bro."

"Get me everything you know about them and email it to the garbage."

"Wait a minute Ram, who found the M&M's first?"

"I did, I'm at the scene of the crime now."

"What color are the M&M's Ram?"

"Green."

"Fuck Ramsey, you've been targeted!"

"Targeted."

"Yeah Ram, so these guys like target like high profile agents. But they don't just target them, they hunt them."

"They've taken Kinkay."

"Fuck, ok you have to search her apartment for clues, well more like bread crumbs."

"I'm not at Kinkay's, I'm at another victim's place."

"Fuck Ram, I need all the facts. Tell me what happened and the order in which you found whatever you found."

Ramsey explained everything that had happened from the moment he'd received the phone call from Matt and Marr. Bringing out every detail he could possibly remember.

"Okay Ram, don't panic, not like you would ever panic, but shit if there were ever a time you did panic, this would be it and I wouldn't judge you," Geeker was sounding excited and nervous at the same time. "She's not dead."

"How do you know Kinkay isn't dead yet?"

"Because there were no M&M's. M&M's are their calling card. Now if they've taken Kinkay then they know she means something to you and they're trying to lure you somewhere. I've been following these guys forever Ram, they make Inferno look like a cupcake. These guys are smart and childish. Have you found a letter, a clue, something?"

"Nothing."

"What about the dog?"

"I'm thinking more that the dog symbolizes how they're going to kill Kinkay if anything."

"Don't sound so fuckin excited."

"I'm sorry Ram, it's just I've been following these guys forever. Anyway there's a bread crumb somewhere at the victim's home. The first clue or puzzle is always a fairly easy one; it should be to like a location or something. They want you to find Kinkay, but they want make a spectacle out of her death to invoke emotion. So, look and look fast, or Kinkay will be on display at the location of that clue. Call me when you've found something."

Geeker disconnected. The M&M killers Ramsey thought, who the fuck are these clowns and what could they want with him. Ramsey walked back into the home, he focused his attention on everything but the scene. Unlike Kinkay's home which had everything turned upside down, the only thing out of place in Cherry's home was the actual murder scene. Ramsey used only his eyes to scan every crevasse of the room.

Nothing stood out of the ordinary to Ramsey. Ramsey checked the kitchen and downstairs area more thoroughly. Ramsey then walked up the stairs to Cherry's bedroom. When Ramsey went to open the door he was met by a little resistance. Ramsey pulled out The Governor before he pushed opened the door. Whatever was behind the door was small and more than one. Ramsey pushed harder and could hear what sounded like small glass statues being knocked to the hardwood floor. Ramsey turned on the light inside of Cherry's room. Her entire room had been converted into a mini world. There were toy houses, buildings, cars. Legos were used to make highways, there was even a downtown area. What threw Ramsey off the most was that all the people were made up of angel statues. The statues ranged from all shapes and sizes and styles, with the exception of one statue which looked more like a wizard to Ramsey. Ramsey's phone rang, it was Geeker.

"You find anything?" questioned Geeker

'Yeah, Chery's room has been turned into some sort of makeshift playhouse."

"How so?"

"The entire room looks like some sort of mini town, with highways and shit. And there's angel statues everywhere. Is there anything in their profile about statue obsessions or angels or any shit like that?" asked Ramsey

"Naw man, you're looking at it wrong. Put on your detective hat, everything is a clue. The room is now just one big clue. So you said there are angel statues everywhere and the room looks like a mini town right?"

Geeker's words drowned out as Ramsey looked at the room through different eyes. His head tilted sideways as he took in the whole room. Geeker's words one big clue resonated through his head.

"Hellooooo," dragged Geeker.

"Not a town, of angels," Ramsey said slowly as his eyes began absorbing the little clues about the room. "It's more like a," Ramsey paused, "a city of angels."

"Okay Geeker, I'm headed to Logan. Tap into the camera system and get footage of any older white males traveling in pairs. Cross reference that with their bank accounts. We're looking for really deep pockets based on those bottles of champagne. Focus on gates with flights coming in from L.A. or connecting flights from L.A.. Book me a flight, I'll call you back in a second."

"Wait a minute Ram, everything I know about the guys says they're still in the state."

"You said follow the bread crumbs right? Well the bread crumbs look like a city of angels.

Ramsey had thought to call Cherry's murder in but he decided not to. He needed her room. Ramsey made his way to his car and pulled out his surveillance kit. Ramsey moved with urgency, taking two steps at a time as he made his way back to Cherry's room. Geeker called while Ramsey was setting up his first camera.

"No flights available, but I did find out that ten minutes from Logan there's a private air strip that caters to the more affluent of customers. That might be a better try."

"Text me the coordinates."

Ramsey hurriedly made his way through the room, taking every bit of precaution to keep the room in perfect condition. Ramsey texted the words "Bird's Eye" to Geeker and then called him to run a quick check on the room before he left.

"We good?" asked Ramsey.

"Perfect."

Ramsey disconnected, by now he already missed five calls from Furnari. The address for the airstrip had already messaged into his phone. Ramsey spoke the coordinates into his Galaxy Note 5 and used his lights as he made his way to the private air strip in 20 minutes flat. The private air strip got Ramsey thinking. If Geeker was right about Kinkay being alive then they were taking Kinkay back to LA, which means they would have to transport a restrained or incapacitated body. Logan airport wouldn't go for that unless it were law enforcement or medically related. Could they be doctors? Are they rolling Kinkay right through Logan? No, the private air strip made more sense. The money that came with the privacy, and confidentiality of the air strip was money well spent.

The gate was secured but Ramsey used his badge to get past the guard. Ramsey pulled up to the main office and made his way inside. An older white gentleman in a suit along with an overweight white male security guard sat in the office.

"Evening gentlemen" started Ramsey.

"May I help you sir?" spoke the man in the suit. The security guard rose at full attention.

Ramsey noticed the large envelope with a few bills protruding out the side lying on the table. His unexpected visit left no time to cover it up. 'The guard out front must not be in on it' thought Ramsey.

"Agent Ramsey here gentlemen. I'm here on a federal matter."

"How can I help?" asked the man in the suit.

"Both of you might be able to help, I need to know of any flights leaving for California within the past two hours, it would be more than likely two males traveling together, but one will do."

"Sorry we haven't had any flights for hour's officer" answered the man in the suit.

"How about you officer?" asked Ramsey

"No sir" said the man with a stern face.

Ramsey looked at both his targets. He analyzed the time he had left to possibly save Kinkay's life, the time it would take to travel to California, plus the time it would take to get these guys to talk. At this rate, Kinkay was already decomposing. 'Time to speed things up' deduced Ramsey. Ramsey pulled his weapon with uncanny speed and fired a round into the knee cap of the security guard. The man in the suit did just what Ramsey figured all his movements and answers said he would. He ran for cover in a nowhere to go situation. Ramsey quickly disarmed the guard of his weapon and ankle holster. He then cuffed him to a metal pole that ran along the base of the wall in the office. Ramsey knew other guards would be coming soon. He only needed a few more seconds. After securing the guard Ramsey made his way to the whimpering man in the suit. Before saying anything Ramsey put the envelope of money in his pocket.

"What do you want?" cried the man.

"Bitch I told you what I want" said Ramsey as he raised his gun.

"Yes, yes, two men, they don't visit very often, blonde haired men. They left over an hour ago."

"Did they have anyone with them?"

"No it was just them."

Just then the guard broke into the room with his gun out.

"Officer" started Ramsey. "I want you to call the Roxbury homicide unit. Ask for Berta Jenkins. Keep an eye on the guard, I need to interrogate this suspect further."

The officer just did as he was told, as Ramsey figured he would. Ramsey took the man in the suit outside of the office.

"Are there any pilots left?" questioned Ramsey.

"No."

"Don't lie to me right now" growled Ramsey as he grabbed the man by his face and slammed his head into the wall. The impact dazed the man causing him to slither to the ground.

"I swear to you, no one is here. They called out of the blue."

"What're their names?"

"I don't know their names, that's why they pay so high."

"And you said it was just the two of them, no one else."

"Yes just the two of them, and a large cargo crate."

"Cargo crate, how large? Big enough to put a person in?"

"I don't know, I mean I suppose."

"I won't bother to ask if you checked."

"Another feature to the price I'm afraid."

Ramsey lifted the man to his feet, cuffed him with zip ties and walked him back to the office.

"Did you get in contact with detective Jenkins?" asked Ramsey to the officer

"Yeah she's on her way."

"Good." Ramsey was running out of time, he needed to get in the air now, just then Ramsey noticed the tattoo on the young officer's neck.

"Hey, where did you serve?" asked Ramsey

"Air force sir, top pilot in my class."

"You can put one these things in the air and make it to California from here."

"I could do that in my sleep."

Ramsey turned to the security guard. "Hey what shoe size you wear tubby?"

Chapter 43

The flight to LA was long but informative. Geeker had sent tons of information on the M&M killers. There was an article that Geeker marked important. It was an article written by a reporter who talked about how he suspected the M&M killers to be involved with countless murders prior to the M&M trademark. He also wrote about how the killers showed a deeper infatuation with hunting the primary investigators on their case, than they did the initial victims. The fact that all the primary investigators were killed two years to the date they were assigned the case to the suspected serial killers didn't sit well with Ramsey. The reporter was never seen again a week after the article was published. Geeker's identifier program was unable to find anyone matching Ramsey's criteria for Kinkay's abductors.

Geeker also sent Ramsey an update on the hunt for Inferno. Vanessa's body had been discovered in the Logan Airport parking lot. Geeker found a match for Michael Sloan as a passenger named James Patterson. Geeker used the identifier program he created to find Officer Sloan. The program identified people based on everything but their face. Geeker sent over a few pictures of the passenger James Patterson. None of the pictures were a clear shot but Ramsey was sure it was Officer Sloan. Ramsey thought about how the M&M killers and the Inferno case were both leading him to L.A. Ramsey didn't believe in coincidences and did he entertain them either. Ramsey knew he was missing a connection he just didn't know what.

Ramsey remotely logged into the surveillance network he'd setup in Cherry's bedroom. Geeker's surveillance program was next level, just like his facial recognition software. Ramsey synced all the cameras he setup to create one picture that he could see and control from every angle. Ramsey was headed to the right city but he needed to figure out where in L.A. and without an actual time clock from the killers, Ramsey had no clue how much time he had left. Ramsey's eyes zoned in on the wizard. Ramsey's days of watching Sesame Street flashed through his mind as Kermit the Frog's "but one of these things just doesn't belong here," chimed in his head. Ramsey tossed the word wizard around his head a few times but nothing popped. Geeker's words banged in his head again, Ramsey zoned in on the location of the wizard. The Lego highways that ran by the wizard was perfect for downtown Los Angeles, and the wizard's position was in a good spot for the Staples Center. Ramsey zoned in closer on the wizard. The statue was perched atop a clock that pointed to 12:55. The globe in the wizard's hand had the tiniest inscription reading the hour is within minutes. Ramsey had no clue what any of this meant, and his brain was on overload, he called Geeker

"You got eyes on the room?" asked Ramsey.

"As we speak," replied Geeker. "So I think I'm still a little stumped on the magician myself, as far as the inscription on the ball is concerned, it doesn't look like its apart of the statue design. When did they make contact with you exactly?"

"Sometime after midnight."

"What's sometime?"

Ramsey checked his call, the call lasted one minute, and he'd received it at 11:59pm.

"11:59, the call lasted one minute, I recorded it, sending it to you now. Ramsey sent the conversation between him and the M&M killers to Geeker and waited while Geeker listened to it.

"Alright, so the tick tock is the definite start of your time clock. You said the call was 11:59 and lasted a minute, your clock started at midnight. Based on the inscription, you have 55 hours from midnight before Kinkay will be on display."

"Ok, but where the fuck is she gonna be?" sighed Ramsey

"It's got something to do with the magician on the watch tower, it's the only statue that isn't an angel"

"Yeah, I'm stumped by this fuckin wizard myself."

"No, it's a magician. You would use wizard in some like fantasy world. The city, although populated by angels, is a real city, so the statue is considered a magician."

"Magician," said Ramsey aloud. "Magician, Magic, Magic, Magician, Staple Center. Magic Johnson, Staples Center. They're gonna display her at the Staple Center."

"It works; Magic Johnson did play for the Lakers. I think we have a winner. Good job Ram."

Ramsey tilted his head back, his mind started to ease. If he couldn't find Kinkay before they killed her, then he could at least catch them while they tried to place her on display, and if things got that far, there was always the hope that they would plan to kill her at the scene as oppose to bringing her there dead. Ramsey thought more about the wizard being a magician and representing Magic Johnson. The wheels in his mind spun for a few moments. It was as if Geeker could hear the actual wheels and pistons going off in Ramsey's head.

"Doesn't Magic Johnson own the L.A. Dodgers or some shit?" asked Ramsey out loud but to himself.

"Co-owner."

Ramsey moved the cameras to where the Dodgers Stadium would be in relation to the Staples Center. An angel stood in the place of Dodger Stadium, as Ramsey zeroed in on the inscription Ramsey immediately noticed that this was no ordinary angel. This was Gabriel, and the inscription read "Messenger of God."

"Okay Geeker, I'll touch back with you when I land. Find me something, anything. Three possible psycho paths in the same city, that's not a coincidence. Anything Geeker"

"Over and out boss."

Ramsey felt like he was flying blind. He needed a break and he needed one fast. Ramsey made a call to a military buddy still in counter intelligence. Ramsey's military friend ran surveillance on all air traffic in and out of California. Besides the regular airlines, only one plane had landed in LA in the past six hours. It had landed on a privately owned strip that catered to the affluent. Ramsey spent nearly the entire flight trying to get clearance at the landing strip without revealing the nature of his request. It had almost taken his onetime and onetime only favor from the President to get the clearance needed. Ramsey made a mental note to himself to use that favor before the next election. Chances of another term for the current President looked bleak.

Ramsey just couldn't fit how the M&M killers tied in with Inferno. Have they been working together the whole time? Was the killing of Vanessa some sort of signal to the M&M killers? Ramsey's head was spinning but at the same time his mind was clear. Although he couldn't focus on one particular subject, his mind seemed to be able to fit perfectly all the pieces he had even with the ones missing.

Once they landed in LA Ramsey made his way to the main control room. He entered the office of the head supervisor in charge. A short Hispanic woman in a gray plaid skirt suit greeted him.

"Detective Ramsey" said the woman as she shook his hand "I'm Mrs. Santiago, sorry for the resistance on the clearance, you have to be aware that we take pride in being of the highest security. Please have a seat."

"I understand," said Ramsey as he declined to sit. "The jet that just recently landed, I need to know the names of the men that were on it."

"What jet are you referring to Officer Ramsey? the services we offer are out of respect."

"I understand; these men may have information on something very important. I need to know where I can find them."

"I'm sorry detective, although you come highly regarded our clients enjoy their privacy."

"And as much as I respect their privacy Mrs. Santiago, a woman's life may very well be in danger by these men."

"I'm sorry detective, I cannot help you, now if you would please excuse me. I'm very busy."

"Of course, can you direct me to the exit? I have a ride picking me up."

"Once you exit the building, head straight to your right."

Ramsey thanked the supervisor and left. He convinced the pilot to stay at the air strip and wait for him. Ramsey had no idea what his next move would be but he wasn't worried, his senses were pulling from too many places for him to miss anything. Once at the gate Ramsey's phone rang.

"Talk to me Geeker," said Ramsey as he exited the main gates to a parking lot for employees and guest. "My next option is putting a gun to the head of a tight lipped Hispanic supervisor. Not that I'd mind that"

"Okay, so after our Michael Sloan now James Patterson lands in LAX we lose him. But not before our friendly cameras catch him chumming it up with one fine piece of tail at the airport and leave with her in a cab. Now after running her face through my little friend here I came back with a Michelle Colby. Now Ms. Colby had reservations at the Marriot in LA. This same Marriot experienced a fire where a woman was found burned to death. In what room I ask? You guessed it, 112, Michelle Colby. Now the police haven't identified her body yet, but we know it's our friend. Now there's actually an ongoing investigation and their trying to identify the man she came in with. I was able to hack into the server that the hotel's cameras feeds up to for storage. Our boy hopped into a cab. From there he took the cab to a bar all the way in Santa Monica. I lose 'em there."

"This doesn't help me find Kinkay."

"You didn't let me finish my good man. The next morning a woman by the name of Sandra Roberts reports her husband Klyde Roberts missing to the police. Of course she has to wait 48 hours, but she reports he went to the same bar that our friend got dropped off to and never came home. According to the bartender the man never came in and when asked to see his camera system he claimed it was just for show and didn't work. I did a little more digging on the owner, turns out he made a purchase for some very high tech surveillance equipment. The funny business is, he used some prepaid card to buy the equipment and pay to have it installed. I would've never made the connection but the cheap bastard used the leftover dollar and sixty-three cents from the prepaid card to pay on his electric bill for the bar. Now why would a bar owner pay all that money for security cameras, have them installed and then not have them working?"

"You've got a point and this is a great reason to go after Inferno, but right now I need to find these fucks holding Kinkay before it's too late."

"How about I give you both. Of all the highest and affluent places to dine in Santa Monica only a few serve Screaming Eagle Cabernet, and this mid-level, blue collared, super surveillance camera, bar happens to be one of them."

"And if we got 'em on camera."

"Then I can tell you who they are."

Chapter 44

Ramsey took a cab from the private air strip. The ride was going to be a while so he decided to make use of his time wisely. Ramsey took out his phone and began swiping through contacts. He found the name he was looking for and dialed.

"I know this is ain't my muthafuckin nigga, what's crackin cuzz?" blared an excited west coast accent through Ramsey's phone.

"Ain't shit, I need a solid from you though. I'm a text you an address. I need you to send two Babysitters," answered Ramsey smoothly.

"Some sitters, oh aight I got u fool. Ey man you this way?"

"Yeah, I'm workin though."

"Fuck all that cuzz, slide through when you get a chance. Oh, I heard da homie got touched. Sorry to hear that."

"Thanks my nig, I gotta go though. Make sure you do that for me though. Oh, send me a pair a workout clothes with them sitters too"

"I got you my nigga, out."

"Peace," ended Ramsey as he began to swipe through his phone again.

"This is Joe," replied a dry distinguished voice.

"Joe muthafuckin show, how's it hangin?"

"Hahahaha," laughed the man loudly. "I haven't been called that in years. Ramsey my man, what the fuck is up?"

"Nothing much man," answered Ramsey in a much softer, lighter, and more professional tone than his previous call. "You still stationed out in LA?"

"Yes sir. You know I'm big Kahuna out here little man."

"As much as I'd like to get into that," laughed Ramsey, "I need to stay focused. I need you to put a surveillance team on the Staples Center and Dodgers Stadium."

"Wait what," cried out Joe in a shocked laugh. "Say that shit again."

"I'm serious Joe," replied Ramsey. The lightness had started to seep out of Ramsey's tone. "And I'm going to need this off the books. I don't know how connected these guys are."

"Shit Ramsey, what's going on? If there's a threat on national soil I can't just run some fuckin under the radar operation to stop it. I gotta get the," Ramsey cut him off.

"It's not a terror threat. Kinkay's been kidnapped and if I can't find the killers in time then one of those places is where I should either find her or my next clue. I'm running this dark, I need you to do the same."

"Fuck Ram."

"Fuck Ram, remember that sweet, gullible, and God awful annoying girl you met right before we came back from leave. And how I covered for you while you banged some broad and her sister. That same girl you married and you told me on your wedding date that you owed me because you love her so much?

"Yeah you told me I didn't owe you shit."

"Fuck you, I lied. I'm calling it in Joe."

"Ramsey I can't. Not without raising some red flags."

"Not my problem at this point. And if for some reason those teams aren't there, I'll ruin you. I'll have Geeker, you remember Geeker right? I'll have Geeker upload one of your video escapades you used to be so proud of. I've got a really good one of you, she couldn't be any more than sixteen if that. I'll have that thing uploaded to every server on this planet for the next twenty-four hours. How long do you think it would be before she leaves you? Or you're fired? Or even arrested? I never liked you Joe you fucking pedophile, and this is not a threat, this a promise/ I'd hoped to use this WMD for something a little more profitable financially. But Kinkay is more important. Get it done," ended Ramsey and then disconnected the call.

The cab driver stared at Ramsey through the rearview mirror. His eyes were a little wide with shock.

"Fuck you lookin at yo? Keep yo shit on the road," barked Ramsey.

The small Asian cab driver placed his eyes back on the road and drove quietly. Ramsey checked his laptop. Geeker had sent him a few emails. He went through them and then closed his laptop. Ramsey's mind was doing so much work his body was drained. For the first time in a long time Ramsey felt like he could walk away from the chess board. He knew his next move; it was only a matter of time. And it wasn't until he actually made his next move would Ramsey be able to revisit the board with a new strategy. So for now Ramsey rested. He closed his eyes and did his best to let go. Before he knew it Ramsey was fast asleep. He dreamt of Cherry. Nothing in the dream was vivid. It was more like a blurred collage of passing images and fragments of time that he'd spent with her. The dream lasted for what seemed like forever.

Chapter 45

Heaven and Michael stood back to take in the view. The spread was magnificent. Heaven had prepared roasted duck with all the trimmings. She said the sauce she made for the duck was a family recipe. The champagne was Clos Du Mesnil, and sitting on ice. The table cloth was made of white silk, and candles brightly burned around the table.

"Just beautiful" said Heaven.

"Let's freshen up before they get here" suggested Michael.

"Race you to the shower" grinned Heaven as she took off down the hallway. "No elevators" she yelled as she rounded the corner that lead to a vast flight of stàirs.

Michael took off after her. Now Michael understood why Heaven drove the way she drove.

That bitch can move Mikey, come on pick it up.

Michael put a little more bounce in his step as he extended his legs to take full strides, using all 4' his legs and waist provided. Michael caught Heaven just as she hit the door and opened it. Without stopping stride, he grabbed her by her waist and took a few steps before he shot her into the air and onto the bed. Michael was in Heaven instantly. The sex was intense and wild. It was as if every thrust and pump connected them even closer. Michael and Heaven went on until they were exhausted.

"I'm going to wash up, I'll call you when the water is hot" said Heaven as she slid out of bed.

Michael watched as Heaven's smoothly shaped ass firmly walked away.

Someone needs to lay off the squats.

And someone could lay off the Twinkies.

You're kidding me right. I'm sculpted like a Greek god. You could wash your panties on this stomach.

Jerk.

Heaven turned the shower on and immediately stepped in. Heaven liked the feeling of a cold shower. It seemed to jolt her back to life. Michael was becoming a drug to her, she enjoyed every minute with him, and couldn't see herself without him now. Matt and Marr were okay, but they seemed juvenile to Heaven. Michael was mysterious, introverted, sexy, confident, and more importantly, like her.

You really like him. Girl talk.

Oh my God Seduce he is so wonderful. He makes me feel warm inside, and mushy. I can't believe this is happening to me.

I'm so happy for you Heaven. You deserve it girl. But that voice of his might be a problem. I don't like him. Where is he anyway?

Heaven could see Michael standing outside of the shower. He was naked and holding something in his hand.

"You gonna come in silly?" asked Heaven.

Michael didn't respond to Heaven he just stood there. Heaven opened the shower door, the knife in Michael's hand caught her a little off guard.

"Michael. What are you doing?" asked Heaven as she began to reach her hand out to Michael.

No Heaven! Don't touch him, don't move.

Seduce immediately noticed the knife in Michael's hand, the bone handle was an image that was seared into Seduce's DNA. Seduce had never seen the knife before but she'd heard stories of its description, power and danger since her creation. Breeders were treated like gods, fearing nothing, nothing except the knife. The handle of the knife was made of bone. No one knew what kind of bone it was, rumors said it was the rib given to Eve from the body of Adam. The blade was made of pure gold with diamonds running along either side. The handle was riddled with random inscriptions and hieroglyphics. The meaning to these inscriptions were just as much a mystery as the knife itself. The history of the blade was a mystery to most voices except Balancers and the one Builder that made it. But the effect of the blade was no mystery. The knife in Michael's hand was the only thing that could kill a Breeder.

He's a Balancer Heaven.

'No he can't be.'

The knife Heaven, there's only one, and it can only be held by a Balancer.

'Then why hasn't he attacked yet?'

I don't know.

Michael just stood there in a trance like state. The knife seemed to glisten without sunlight.

"Michael babe, it's me, Heaven. Put the knife down babe. It's okay." Heaven stepped out of the shower and towards Michael.

No Heaven don't.

Heaven ignored Seduce and continued to approach Michael.

Don't touch the knife.

"Michael, Michael" said Heaven as she drew closer to him.

KILL HER, KILL HER NOW MICHAEL.

Don't do it Mikey, she's got answers.

DO IT MICHAEL, KILL HER. KILL HER NOW MICHAEL, DO IT NOW!!

Heaven touched Michael's wrist. The touch brought Michael out of the trance. The knife dropped from his hand, clanging to the floor.

"What, what happened?" questioned Michael.

"Nothing baby let's just get dressed. Matt and Marr will be here soon."

Michael noticed the knife on the floor.

"Whose is that?" asked Michael.

"Don't worry about that. I'll have Suela pick it up later."

Heaven hurried Michael out of the bathroom and closed the door. The two of them dressed in an awkward silence. Just as Michael gained the courage to break the silence a Beethoven tune chimed throughout the house.

"They're here Michael. We have to hurry. We'll talk about this later."

Chapter 46

Ramsey had given the cabbie an address a few blocks away from the actual bar in order to cover his tracks. Ramsey secured his travel kit on his back and made his way to the bar. The sun had just set and the breeze from the coast felt amazing to him. Ramsey's phone buzzed with a text simply stating, 'here'. Ramsey arrived at the bar. He knew his two Babysitters wouldn't know him right away so Ramsey walked over to a pay phone next to the bar and stood in his best Crip stance. In a matter of seconds two very large older looking black males exited a car. Ramsey gave them the signal to wait there and walked over to the men.

"Okay fellas," started Ramsey as one of the men handed him a mask a set of gloves and a firearm. "Follow my lead, no fireworks unless we're taking fire. Understood."

The Babysitters nodded yes before putting on their mask and gloves. Ramsey walked into the bar first. The place was small. Ramsey was thankful only three pedestrians were in the bar and the owner. Ramsey recognized the owner from one of the emails Geeker had sent which possessed a picture of the owner, along with a small bio. The owner was Tim Stall a tall white male with sandy brown hair and a fish hooked nose. He was middle aged and divorced with no kids. Ramsey didn't ponder on the owner's connection to the killers, he intended to get all his answers straight form the horse's mouth.

"I wanna see hands people," yelled Ramsey at the top of his lungs while pointing his gun. The Babysitters locked the door and turned over the closed sign after they entered. Ramsey and the owner locked eyes.

"Don't you move Mr. Stall," snarled Ramsey while he pointed his gun straight at the owner and headed directly towards him.

"Hey, I don't want any trouble. We're just opening up. I don't have a lot a cash. But take what you want."

"What I want," said Ramsey once he got close enough to the owner to place the barrel of his gun to the owner's head, "is information."

Ramsey grabbed the owner by the collar.

"Back office, now," said Ramsey as he pushed the owner.

The owner stumbled towards the back office, Ramsey closed the door behind him.

"What do you want man?"

Ramsey butted the owner in the nose with his gun handle. Blood instantly poured from the man's nose. The owner covered his nose as he coward in pain.

"I want access to your surveillance system."

"I don't have a surveillance system," cried the man

Ramsey let off a round next to the man's ear and into the wall.

"Fuuuck," yelled the man.

"I won't ask again. It'll take a little longer but I can do this without you."

"Okay, okay. What do you want me to do?"

Ramsey pulled out his cellphone put it on speaker and placed it on a night stand.

"Yello."
"I'm with the owner and the security system, whadda ya need?"

"Okay, have him log in and then put his network online, he must be running it on an offline terminal which is why I can't get in," answered Geeker

"You heard the nerd. Sit down and type"

The owner put his network online and in minutes Geeker was in. Ramsey placed his travel kit on the table and removed a picture of Michael from his kit. Ramsey walked over to the owner who was still putting the network online and placed the photo on the table. Ramsey backed up a few paces and waited for Geeker to connect.

"I'm in," announced Geeker.

"I'm gonna leave the line open," said Ramsey to Geeker. "The man in the photo," started Ramsey to the owner "have you seen 'em before?"

After a quick glance the owner quickly replied no.

"Okay I'm putting images up now from that night on the screen. There's Michael up top, and next to him is our missing Klyde Roberts. The Woman in the middle row is Heaven Dubois. Her assets range in the multi-millions. I couldn't find any address or anything for her in L.A. or Santa Monica, or anywhere else in California for that matter. She's who Michael left with. The bottom row are other patrons there that night while the others up top were present. The first two are my favorite for Mr. Roberts's disappearance, they followed him out of the bar after some sort of verbal altercation."

"Fuck you mean sort of a verbal altercation."

"This security system has great audio; I was able to pick up Mr. Robert's insulting the men. He called them and I quote 'fucking faggots' the weird part is though, the men just whistled. I mean literally that's what they did all night is whistle like it was some sort of language to them. Well anyway, after that Mr. Roberts leaves after a short while, and they follow. Their names are Mathew Kingsley and Marrtheus Underwood. It looks like they went to Yale together. After school they both just kind of disappeared. No paper trail, no assets, nothing it's like they, they vanished. Around the same time the M&M murders started."

"Those two men," said Ramsey as he pointed at the two men on the bottom row to the far left of the screen. "Are they the ones drinking Screaming Eagle Cabernet? Now before you answer, you've already lied to me once. I won't tolerate it again."

"Yes, they order it. I serve it only for them."

"Is Ms. Dubois picking up their tab?"

"Yes."

"What do you know about her?"

"I don't know anything; she barely talks to me. She just pays their tabs, I swear."

Ramsey stepped back and fired a round in the owner's far right shoulder. The impact of the weapon knocked the owner out of his seat.

"I guess you don't understand how this works. Information is what keeps you alive. Soooooo," smiled Ramsey as he took off his mask. "The lack there of will only make this worse," continued Ramsey. Ramsey eyes had become menacing, he wanted the man to see how far this could go. "Now you wouldn't lie to police just to protect a good paying customer. What is this some sort of feeding ground?" growled Ramsey as he raised his gun to the man again and stepped forward

"Alright, alright. They pay me for silence. I don't say anything to anyone about anything. Ms. Dubois likes her privacy."

"And the two fuckin faggots?"

"They're never any trouble. That's like the first time something like this is ever happened where someone's gone missing. That's all I know I swear."

Ramsey's bull shit meter wasn't going haywire but something else was telling him to push. He'd come too far. The man had crawled the wall to a stance by now. Ramsey looked away, keeping the man in sight through the corner of his eye. In chess sometimes recklessness can scare a weaker opponent who is at an advantage and doesn't know it. Ramsey turned back to the owner and fired a bullet into his leg. The owner screamed in agony as he crashed to the floor. Ramsey quickly made his way over to the owner and grabbed him by his throat forcing him to his feet as he slammed him against the wall. The owner gagged on his own spit as his head collided with the wall. Ramsey rested the barrel of his gun square in the eye socket of the owner. Giving it just enough pressure for the owner to acknowledge that this was it.

"Where can I find them?" asked Ramsey quietly. Ramsey applied a little pressure to the man's throat.

The man began to sob. As he racked his brain for something anything to give Ramsey worth letting him live.

"I don't," started the man.

Before he could say anything else Ramsey moved the gun adjacent to the man's head and fired four rounds in a quick concession. The sound frightened the man to the point where his body jerked frantically but Ramsey held firmly as he quickly placed the guns barrel back on the man's eye socket.

"Tell me something, take as much as you need to think before you speak your next words," said Ramsey coldly.

The owner was beside himself with grief. His eye was in so much pain from the heat of the barrel. He could feel it swelling shut. The owner had no clue what to do, his mind raced for anything that could save his life.

"Okay Geeker he's useless."

"Waaait," yelled the owner.

"Get ready Geeker, he's gonna give us something we can use."

A light bulb went off in the owner's head.

"Okay, okay. One night she took a cab. She drove here like she usually does. But she was really fuckin sad like crying and shit. I closed the whole place down and just let her fucking cry.

"What was she crying about?"

"Some guy, some guy named fucking Tabias. She just kept saying his name over and over."

"What about 'em?"

"I don't fuckin remember," sobbed out the owner. "I think he died or something. Or like she was crying about him being dead or some shit." The owner's legs kept giving way but Ramsey wouldn't let him fall. "Anyway she got too wasted to drive. In all the years she's been coming here she's never gotten that fucked up. I called her a cab home."

"Where?" asked Ramsey with excitement climbing in his voice.

"Somewhere far along the coast. I don't remember where exactly."

Ramsey pressed the gun hard against the owner's eye.

"That's all I know that's all I know!" screamed the man. "I swear that's all I know. I only remember because they made her pay something crazy like a hundred dollars in advance. It was like over a year ago. I swear I don't know shit else," cried the owner hysterically.

"Fuck Ram, they killed everyone," said a Geeker with a surprisingly shocked tone.

"Killed who Geeker?"

"The cab company he called for her. They torched it. Every current employee at that time has gone missing or has been found dead, or brutally murdered. There are literally no financial records, no taxes filed, nothing about this place ever existing on paper can be found. Apparently there wasn't a lot of coverage on the story. The family of the employees made a little noise but that noise died out after a while. I managed to compile a photo array of every employee working at that time. Whoever wiped their records is good. You're gonna have to see if our friend over there was a gentleman and walked her to the cab"

The photos hit the screen as Ramsey swung the man around and threw him back in front of the computer. The owner sobbed quietly as he scanned the photos. Ramsey waited quietly, the suspense was killing him.

"Him, him right there," pointed the owner with his good arm.

"Third row from the bottom Geeker two from the right."

"Jean Baptist, he and his wife were found stabbed to death in their home. Their daughter Natalia was placed in a psychiatric ward shortly thereafter. Nothing in the police reports about why really, but she was a registered nurse at the time, it would've taken something dramatic to unhinge her like that. Luckily her doctor logs all his note into a computer. She's been in session with the good doctor for over five months, and according to these notes, she's only uttered two words. Tick Tock."

Chapter 47

Geeker had found an address for Natalia's ex-boyfriend along with a picture and bio on the ex-boyfriend. Alfonso Gray AKA AG a member of the blood gang held an extensive police record ranging from violence to narcotics possession. Geeker found some other charges on Alfonso that mysteriously were dropped, Ramsey had a good idea why. According to Ramsey's gps the ex-boyfriend would be a stop they could make on the way. When they pulled up to the neighborhood the Babysitter's mood instantly changed. Ramsey could see the Babysitter's body language become more aggressive. They had pulled into a Blood neighborhood. The cul-de-sac was located in the back of a maze of turns Ramsey had to take to get to the ex-boyfriend's home. The Babysitter wasn't wearing any colors and he wasn't flagging. The Babysitter not wearing anything that would represent his Crip affiliation would work in their favor, and with any luck they would make it out of here without incident.

The house they pulled up to was run down, surrounded by more run down homes. The black steel mesh covering the door hung by one hinge. There was no porch and no steps, just a slab of concrete you stepped on like a stool to enter the front door. Young black men and women peppered all throughout the cul-de-sac, each little group engaged in their own current situation but all unified by one color, red.

Ramsey placed the car in park and looked at the Babysitter, "you staying in the car?" asked Ramsey.

"Naw cuzz."

The two men exited the vehicle, Ramsey secured his travel kit on his back before proceeding to the door. The arrival of Ramsey and the Babysitter had drawn the attention of the entire cul-de-sac; all eyes were on them. Ramsey put on his cop hat, it was the best way out of this situation in his mind. Ramsey tapped on the hanging mesh several times, he could hear N.W.A coming from the house. The door cracked opened but it didn't open all the way, it was still locked from the inside with a chain lock.

"Who 'da fuck is you blood? And why 'da fuck you bangin on my doh?" said the man behind the door.

Ramsey could tell it was Alfonso from the image Geeker had sent, "Mr. Gray, I'm detective Ramsey, I just need to ask you a few questions about Natalia, I'll only be a moment," said Ramsey.

"Fuck outa here blood, I don't talk to cops," replied Alfonso.

"Well me and you both know that's not true," whispered Ramsey through the door. "And unless you talk to me, so will everyone else. Just a couple questions, nothing else."

Alfonso stared at Ramsey coldly. The smell of alcohol wafted from Alfonso's breathe while the smell of marijuana stormed out of the house. He looked towards the Babysitter and then back at Ramsey. The door closed and within a few seconds Ramsey could hear the chain lock sliding. Alfonso opened the inner door, swinging it to himself, he then used his hands to motion for Ramsey to step back. After stepping back Alfonso gave a swift kick to the bottom outer corner of the black steel mesh. The meshed door popped open and swung by Ramsey's face and Alfonso stepped aside for them to step up and walk in.

The house was a two story, Alfonso pointed them to the living room. The place was an utter mess, Ramsey nor the Babysitter bothered to sit down. A white girl laid sprawled out on the couch half naked. She was a pretty brunette who just looked high and in need of some water. The small table was cluttered with cigar guts from rolling blunts. Miscellaneous scraps of papers and receipts were scattered all over the place and on the table was a sawed off shotgun sat atop the table. The handle was wrapped in gray duct tape that was colored red.

"What you got to ask Blood?" questioned Alfonso.

"What happened between you and Natalia?"

"Fuck you mean what happened nigga, da' bitch went nuts. Dis' nigga," chuckled Alfonso.

"Why she go crazy, what happened before that?"

"I don't fuckin know, da' bitch wasn't wit me when she lost her shit. She was over by her sister house."

"What're you talking about?" asked Ramsey

"Me and the bitch was fightin, she went over her sister's house, next time I see the bitch she in a stray jacket. All she kept saying was tick tock and left right left type shit."

"Left right left?" asked Ramsey with a puzzled look to match his puzzled tone.

"Yeah nigga, left right left. I mean sometimes she say left twice or right twice but that's all she was saying."

"Did you speak to her prior to the murders while she was over her sister's house?"

"Yeah."

"What did you talk about, think."

"I don't know nigga, dumb shit like, like gettin back togetha and shit like that. Regular shit."

"Think nigga, she didn't talk about her day? She ain't tell you what she' been up to? Or where you just not listenin?"

"Nigga, all she did was sleep and cry and text me."

"You sure? You sure she wasn't seein no one else?"

"Nigga is you stupid, that bitch was on my dick. Like I said, all she did was cry, sleep and text me. Every time I hit her up she was at the house, ok one time she left. She went wit her dad out by the coast somewhere. That's the only shit she did nigga. Fuck you mean my bitch was seein someone. Nigga you must be out yo rabbit ass mind, that bitch love me to this day."

"Where by the coast?"

"Nigga I don't know. All Nat kept saying was," Alfonso paused when he said Nat, the memories of him and Natalia flooded his soul. Alfonso began to tear up, "Nat, you know, I was the only person she let call her Nat. She had a way of," Alfonso paused again and looked off to the side to hide his tears.

"I know," said Ramsey. "I just wanna help make this right."

"How," said Alfonso with tears and a look of disbelief. "How the fuck you gonna make it right blood?"

"By bringing the men who killed her parents to justice, now tell me where she went."

"I told you I don't know. She just said by the coast somewhere. Her dad was taking her to see a house or some shit. Some bitch he dropped off. I guess the house was the dopest shit the nigga ever seen or suttin. I don't know where though, Nat was always good wit directions. She had some like built in GPS in her head or suttin, she was like, hol'a fuck up blood, I know you ain't bring no hardback in my muthafuckin spot?"

Ramsey noticed it as well, at some point Babysitter got comfortable and forgot they were both deep undercover. The Babysitter had become relaxed and without being conscious of it had placed his feet in the stance of a Crip. The stance was second nature to him like breathing, and now the cat was out of the bag.

"Nigga I asked you a question," said Alfonso as he began to take steps towards the table.

"Don't do that," exclaimed Ramsey as he quickly drew his weapon and took a step back.

"Oh it's like that?" smiled Alfonso as he shook his head.

"Relax, we ain't here on that shit. This is about Nat."

"Don't you fuckin say her name," screamed Alfonso.

"Okay, I get it. We're leaving." Ramsey kept his gun and eyes on Alfonso as he reached behind his back and unzipped a pocket located at the bottom of his travel pack. A small blue tooth ear piece landed in his hand. Ramsey clicked the button on the side of the blue tooth and placed it in his ear.

"Yo," answered Geeker.

"Extraction, possibly hostile."

"On it," replied Geeker.

Ramsey placed his full attention back on Alfonso "Now we're just gonna walk outa here nice and quietly. No one has to get hurt."

"Oh really?" replied Alfonso

"Really," retorted Ramsey as he placed the sawed off in the front of his trousers. Ramsey fished in his pocket and tossed the Babysitter the key.

"What makes you think I won't just tell the homies as soon as you hop in yo ride to light yo shit up," stated Alfonso.

"Because you're not smart enough to explain to the cops or the rest of our blood buddies out there why a cop and a Crip was in your house moments before they were killed," replied Ramsey smugly.

Alfonso stared at Ramsey with venom. Ramsey was not aware of just how deeply Alfonso hated Crips. The Babysitter was the first out the door while Ramsey kept his weapon trained on Alfonso. Ramsey put his gun away before he exited the home. The natives were paying very close attention to Ramsey and the Babysitter now. Just as Ramsey opened his door to the car Alfonso flew open the door screaming that he'd been robbed. Ramsey saw the automatic handgun in Alfonso's hand raising and wasted no time dispatching Alfonso's soul to heaven or hell, Ramsey never judged.

The first bullet struck Alfonso in the stomach, causing Alfonso to drop his gun and stumble back a bit. The second shot came seconds after and struck Alfonso in the head. Alfonso collapsed shockingly quickly to his knees as if his body had become one long cooked noodle. His body crashed out of the home, Alfonso's feet were still in the doorway as Alfonso laid face first in front of his home.

Bullets engulfed the car, and before Ramsey knew it, he was staring at a dead Babysitter. Ramsey got as low as he could behind the car door while under fire.

"They're starting to surround you Ram, you gotta move. They're heavy on your left," warned Geeker.

Ramsey made a move for Alfonso's house. Ramsey pulled the sawed off shotgun from his and fired both slugs towards the band of thugs pressing on his left as he made his way to Alfonso's doorway. Shots flew everywhere by Ramsey as he dove into the home. Ramsey tried to close the door with his feet quickly but Alfonso's feet were blocking the door. Ramsey scurried over to Alfonso's feet and pushed them out the way and slammed the door shut. Bullets shook the frame of the house as Ramsey crawled to the living room. The brunette was gone, Ramsey figured she took off once the shooting started. Ramsey wiped his prints from the shotgun and threw the gun by the door.

"Out the back door and to the right. Don't stop hopping walls until I tell you. And be fast about, it looks like reinforcements are gearing up," said Geeker

Ramsey wasted no time fleeing for the back door. Ramsey bolted off to his right. The wall that Ramsey was approaching divided the houses and was only six feet high. Ramsey's blur alerted his pursuers as he flew by. Ramsey stopped a few inches before he ran into the wall and leaped almost straight in the air, slightly leaning his weight towards the wall. Instead of grabbing for the wall Ramsey kicked off the wall propelling himself above the wall. As his feet pass the wall Ramsey used his hands to grab the other side of the wall and pulled his body over. The move was quick and precise. Ramsey followed this pattern over three more walls, the Bloods just couldn't keep up with Ramsey.

"Okay Ram after this next wall you're gonna jump the back wall. It's gonna put you in an alley big enough to fit a car. You're gonna head right once you're in the alley, about a quarter mile down you're gonna come to a four-way intersection, take that left and your home free."

Ramsey was clearing the back wall and doing a mental check on his ammo when Geeker spoke of being home free. Seven bullets left counted Ramsey. Ramsey had more firepower in his pack but he was hoping he wouldn't have to use that just yet.

"Now I'm getting small activity in the alleyway. Can't really tell if there hostile or not, just be cautious," finished Geeker.

Ramsey could hear the cars in traffic off to his left as he sprinted down the alleyway. The alleyway was dark; all the alley lights had been busted out. It was hard for Ramsey to see much in front of him and the alley slightly curved. Ramsey's heart was encouraged when he saw blips of light hit the intersection of the alley. Ramsey could see the intersection in full view now and the blips of light were much bigger now. Ramsey noticed a car parked on the opposite side of the intersection. The car wasn't what caught Ramsey's attention, it was the silhouette of a man holding what looked to be a fully automatic weapon laying on the roof the car. Ramsey slowed all the way down to a walk, lining up the man on the roof of the car and the passenger. Ramsey moved his weapon back and forth between the two nonstop. Ramsey began to pick up pace never stopping his repetition of aiming back and forth between targets. As Ramsey approached the intersection, headlights flooded the alleyway as the driver threw on his high beams. The lights caught Ramsey off guard but he never broke pattern, instead when the lights boomed Ramsey fired four shots at the gunner on the roof and three shots at the passenger. The man on the roof of the car never even got a chance to let off a shot.

"Three down none to go," laughed Geeker.

"Not yet," chuckled Ramsey.

Ramsey bolted towards the car at top speed while pulling out the Governor from the small of his back. The driver was so shocked by the recent turn of events that he forgot he had his seatbelt on while trying to get out of the car. As Ramsey approached the driver grew more and more frightened, unbuckling his seatbelt became a task of unbearable complexity. Finally, in a fit of desperation the driver grabbed for the passenger's weapon and started firing out the front window. Maybe had he tried this plan when Ramey was a little further out he would've had better success. Ramsey shot a round through the windshield of the car. The bullet crashed through like a linebacker on a blitz striking the driver in the chest. The gun flailed in his arms as he jerked back from the impact. The chest wound hadn't killed him but Ramsey was on top of him now. Ramsey ran up the hood of the car, and onto the roof. He stopped above the man's head and let the Governor off three times.

Everything had become silent, Ramsey could feel his heart racing. Ramsey put away The Governor and his empty weapon, he looked down at the corpse that lay on the roof of the car. Ramsey slowly walked back down the hood of the car and looked back at the carnage before he stepped down. Ramsey was in the middle of a shit storm, he blamed it all on Officer Sloan. Ramsey didn't know how, but he knew Officer Sloan was the reason Cherry had been killed, Kinkay was being held hostage or worse, and all the laws Ramsey was now breaking and people he had recently killed were all because of Officer Michael Sloan.

Ramsey made his way to the main street, he debated on stealing a car or flagging a cab. Ramsey figured he'd broken enough laws in the past half hour, no need for an unnecessary one. Ramsey caught the one break he was begging for all night. An empty cab was passing by, Ramsey flagged the cab down and just his luck the driver stopped. Ramsey hopped in and instructed the big African driver who introduced himself as Matufu to take him to the psychiatric ward on Santa Monica Boulevard.

Geeker emailed Ramsey a dossier on Natalia Baptist that Ramsey went over thoroughly as he rode to the hospital. The reports from her doctor showed no promise in Natalia, but the reports did show a big effort on the doctor's part. The doctors did everything to try and figure out what Natalia meant with her ramblings. They took her on car rides and followed her directions, they brought in different pictures of clocks to see if the images triggered anything. All this after months of constant therapy sessions, no one could reach Natalia. Ramey sent word for reinforcements for the Babysitter he left watching the bar and he reported the loss of the other Babysitter. Frustration and anxiety curled in the pit of Ramsey's stomach. He seemed so close to Kinkay and yet so far.

Chapter 48

Ramsey pulled up to the Santa Monica psychiatric ward and instructed the cab driver to keep the meter running. It was after visiting ours and Ramsey still didn't have a plan on how he was going to get an audience with Natalia. Ramsey's Boston police badge got him past the not to attentive security guard. Ramsey knew Natalia was on the 5th floor in room 511 based on the dossier he received from Geeker. Ramsey took the elevator up to the 5th floor. He exited to a small hallway that led him to a steel bolted door with a lady behind a counter to buzz you in and out.

"Excuse me sir, visiting hours are over," said the lady as Ramsey approached.

The woman was Spanish with long dark flowing hair. She was of a short stature with a pudgy little brown face.

"I'm sorry," started Ramsey as he continued to walk towards her. "I'm detective Ramsey, and I'm here to see a patient of yours," Ramsey was now in front of the woman giving his million-dollar smile.

"Do you have a warrant, or some sort of court order?"

"The woman I need to see is Natalia Baptist. Please I just need a few minutes of her time," replied Ramsey.

"Yes, but do you have a warrant?"

"No, I do not."

"I'm sorry officer, without a warrant I can't let you back there."

"Okay, okay look I get it, you have rules to follow. But there is a child's life that is in danger, and Natalia Baptist might be the only one that can save them," Ramsey knew kids were always a stronger puller when it came to strings of the heart.

"I'm sorry detective, as bad as it makes me feel, I can't help without some sort of legal document."

Ramsey could see the softness in her eyes grow softer, he pushed further. Ramsey pulled out his wallet and showed a picture of his youngest boy. "They have my son, please just a few minutes. Please."

The woman looked at him, Ramey's performance was Emmy worthy.

"Three minutes' detective," said the woman as she buzzed the door. "I don't know if Natty will be of much help, she only says a couple of words."

"Thank you, thank you so much," exclaimed Ramsey as he opened the door.

The woman pulled down a gate that closed the space between her and the hallway. She placed a pad lock on the gate, and locked the buzzer to the door with another key.

"This way detective," said the woman as she walked Ramsey to Natalia's room. Once they reached Natalia's room, the receptionist used another key to unlock the door.

"Natty doesn't really sleep much," said the woman to Ramsey before opening the door. "Hey Natty, you have a visitor." The woman looked back at Ramsey and said "I'll be right outside," and closed the door behind Ramsey.

Natalia was staring out the window. She was fully clothed but still bore a bathrobe. Her hair was long and wild. She stood at about 5'6' and couldn't weigh any more than 120 pounds to Ramsey. The lighting to the room was dim, giving a gloomy feeling to the room. There were no padded walls, but the stale pale cream colored walls didn't help the ambience. One table, a dresser, and a bed furnished Natalia's room. The bed was perfectly made and the table was neatly arranged with different kinds of whistles.

Ramsey set his travel kit down and withdrew his laptop. He booted up his laptop and the noise gained Natalia's attention. She looked at Ramsey's face. Ramsey returned the stare, he could see emptiness in her eyes. Ramsey put together the turn of events that lead Natalia here. He was positive Natalia had witnessed her parent's murder and that whatever she saw ripped the soul out of her. While the laptop booted Ramsey dialed in Geeker through his earpiece.

"I need you on Audio," ordered Ramsey.

"Roger that," replied Geeker.

Ramsey pulled up the images of Matt and Marr but he didn't show them to her, instead he kept the laptop facing himself and stood up with it in his hands.

"Hello Natalia. I'm John. Is it ok for us to talk Natalia?" said Ramsey.

"Tick Tock," answer Natalia dryly.

"Tick Tock," repeated Ramsey aloud. "Did someone say that to you?"

"Tick Tock."

"Natalia, I want to show you something."

"Tick Tock."

Ramsey walked up to Natalia and showed her the images of Mat and Marr. Natalia's reaction to Matt and Marr took Ramsey by surprise. Ramsey was expecting, hoping for her to scream in shock of seeing her parent's killer or start ranting frantically, something anything emotional. Instead Natalia had become very quiet, she gazed at the images and drew closer. She caressed their faces on the screen and began to whistle, the tune took both Geeker and Ramsey by surprise.

"Is she whistling Highway to Hell?" asked Geeker.

Ramsey willed Geeker to shut up as he focused on Natalia.

"Natalia, Natalia," repeated Ramsey but Natalia just kept whistling. "Nat," said Ramsey. Natalia stopped whistling and looked

Ramsey in his eyes. "Nat," repeated Ramsey, "I need your help, where did you see these men?"

Terror suddenly gripped Natalia as she backed away screaming left right erratically. The nurse quickly unlocked the door.

"You have to leave."

"Stay put Ram," said Geeker

"Sir you have to leave, if you don't leave I will be forced to call security."

"Call em," responded Ramsey.

The woman pulled out her walkie- talkie and radioed for security while she went to unlock the gate and the buzzer. Ramsey packed up his laptop and waited patiently for security while Natalia continued to rant out left right. After a few minutes' security arrived.

"I'm leaving," said Ramsey with his hands in the air.

The security guard escorted Ramsey out, the guard was mad a first but Ramsey managed to win him back over by the time they arrived downstairs.

Once in the cab Ramsey pulled out his laptop and began to work with Geeker.

"Where to?" asked Motufu.

"Gimmie a sec brotha, I'm working on that.

"So what're you thinking Ram?"

"Okay so I'm seeing Mr. Baptist taking Heaven home the night she was too drunk to drive. Mr. Baptist is so impressed with the house he takes his daughter to see it, they probably go at night. They run into Matt and Marr at the residence. There's an exchange of some kind between them and Matt and Marr do their whistling shit, but I'm thinking they never got a really good look at Natalia. Later Matt and Marr kill the husband and the wife mistaking the wife for Natalia. And Natalia witnessed the whole thing. And who knows, maybe they whistled the whole time or said tick tock while doing the shit."

"You got a sick fucking mind bro, but why kill all the other employees?"

"Mr. Baptist has a big mouth maybe?"

"And what about the left right?"

"The left right is a map to Matt and Marr."

"Yeah but they tried that, it was a dead end."

"First off if you mean 'they' as in that half ass staff, you gotta be shitting me. And plus I bet they didn't run the coordinates through some super computer starting from the murder scene."

"No they did not. I already started breaking down the left right pattern from the time you left the room, every forty-five seconds the pattern starts over. So based on the description of the drive from the bartender and Alfonso and the upfront charge for the cab we end up at one address on Ocean Avenue. According to state and town records the house is not for sale and uninhabited, but I'm picking up movement. I got seven warm bodies, five of them are in a cluster."

When the confirmation of the house being on Ocean Avenue came through, something about the city of clues left in Chery's home stabbed at Ramsey.

"I'm sending you the coordinates to the address now," said Geeker.

Ramsey pulled up the cameras set up in Cherry's bedroom and focused on the part of the city that would've ran along the coast of Santa Monica. Every angel statue that covered Ocean Avenue was a baby cherub, all except one. Ramsey zoomed in on the name inscribed at the bottom of the angel statue, it simply read "Cardea."

"Cardea," read Ramsey aloud

"Did you say Cardea? As in the goddess of protecting the home," said Geeker.

"Yuuup," said Ramsey softly as he tapped the screen. "We're going to a goddess.

Chapter 49

Ramsey planned his point of attack during the entire cab ride to the mansion. Ramsey instructed the driver to pull over about a mile from the mansion. He gave the driver a thousand dollars out of the envelope he'd taken.

While showing the cab driver his badge Ramsey said "I want you to call an ambulance in the next twelve minutes, and the police in fifteen."

"Is everything okay sir, please I don't want any trouble my friend."

"No, no trouble for you Motufu,' just do as I say, and everything will be fine"

"Ok my friend."

"Good. Keep the meter running."

"What I say to the ambulance?"

"Tell them an officer is hurt and needs help."

"And the police?"

"Tell them an officer has been shot."

Ramsey exited the cab with his travel kit in hand. After serving so many years as a SEAL being prepared was just something hardwired into Ramsey's way of thinking. Ramsey's travel kit contained the bare essentials to keep the weight light. A small lap top with a satellite chip for internet access, a satellite phone, two handguns, an HK MP7 with two clips, a few flash bangs, a couple of grenades, a lock pick, a flashlight, some passports, and a wad of cash. The cash part had just increased by a few thousand which was never a bad thing. The jog to the outer fence was quick and paced perfectly. Ramsey didn't feel the slight bit winded, Ramsey hoped it was due to his great shape, but chances were his adrenaline had a lot more to do with it. He made the run in a little over 5 minutes, the world record was about fifteen seconds under four minutes, give or take a second.

Ramsey downloaded blue prints of the mansion while riding in the cab. His point of entrance was going to be the service entrance to the rear of the home. The only variables Ramsey had to worry about were security, pets, and staff.

After scaling the twelve-foot iron fence that surrounded the mansion. Ramsey made his way to the rear. It appeared to be empty of security or unfriendly animals. Ramsey observed a woman in a maid's uniform through the service entrance door. From the shadows he could see she was pouring glasses of something. Ramsey counted five glasses.

Chapter 50

"So glad that you could join us. Please, have a seat," gleamed Matt as Heaven and Michael entered the room.

"What a lovely spread you've prepared Ms. Heaven, wouldn't you agree Dr. Kinkay?" said Marr.

Kinkay was at a loss for words. The sight of Officer Sloan was more than she could handle. It's not the fact that Ramsey was right about Officer Sloan that scared Kinkay, it was that now she was face to face with the monster. The monster that devoured all its victims.

"Well don't be rude Dr. Kinkay. Speak," ordered Matt.

"Now who's being rude? You haven't even introduced us," injected Heaven.

"Well Michael needs no introduction. Isn't that right Officer Sloan?" grinned Marr.

Heaven looked accusingly at Michael and Dr. Kinkay. "You know this woman Michael?" questioned Heaven.

"Please, please, you're ruining the dinner conversation," said Matt sternly. "Now why don't we all just sit down, Suela is bringing in the champagne. Great selection I might add."

Chapter 51

Ramsey stood silently by the door that lead to the dining area, his travel kit with the exception of his lap top, SAT phone, and HK were now on his waist. The HK rested lightly on Ramsey's back, harnessed by a shoulder strap. Ramsey had already concluded that he didn't have the time or the risk factor to see if the maid would cooperate. Suela walked pass Ramsey, but she picked up on his presence a second too late. Ramsey put Suela in a sleeper hold. Suela bucked forward, giving Ramsey a stronger tug than he expected. Ramsey squeezed harder, he had to take Suela out without killing her or making any noise, but it was turning out to be more difficult than anticipated.

At the point of increased pressure Suela rocked her whole body forward, taking Ramsey right off his feet. The move surprised Ramsey, but he quickly latched his legs around her body to keep from flipping over. 'What the fuck is up with is bitch' thought Ramsey. Then Suela did something even more unexpected, she jumped clean in the air with Ramsey on her back.

"Fuck this." Ramsey snapped Suela's neck midair. The fall to the ground created an awfully loud thud.

Chapter 52

"Did you hear that?" questioned Marr as he rose from the table.

"Suela! Suela dear, are you alright?" yelled Heaven

"Come let's see if she's okay" said Matt rising."

Chapter 53

With no time to waste Ramsey slung his HK from his back and into an aimed position and headed for the door. Ramsey's first instinct was to throw a flash bang in the room as he placed hi HK on single fire. But he had no time to get an idea of the seating position, a flash bang may help but if one of the killers were near Kinkay, they might kill her before Ramsey could save her.

"Hands where I can see 'em," said Ramsey as he kicked in the door training his weapon on each potential target and then finally resting on Michael.

"Detective, how good of you to join us" cheesed Marr uncontrollably.

Matt quickly slid behind Kinkay who was sitting to his right, instinctively Ramsey placed Matt into his crosshairs. The knife came out so quickly you would think it instantly materialized. Matt caressed Kinkay's face with the blade of the knife while slightly combing his fingers through her hair at the same time. The blade had already nicked her neck, causing red hot blood to flow. You could actually feel the temperature rise as the presence of fresh blood hit the air.

"Now is that anyway a respected guest should act?" whispered Matt into Kinkay's ear loud enough for Ramsey to hear. "Put the gun down detective."

"That's not gonna happen," replied Ramsey.

"Then I guess where going to have to watch Dr. Kinkay bleed to death," replied Marr.

Now this is a dinner party. Grab a roll Mikey, get comfy.

Michael stood to reach over for a roll. Ramsey trained his gun on him without thought.

"Easy detective, I'm just getting a roll," grinned Michael as he stood arms wide showing his dinner roll.

In any other situation Ramsey would've played it calm and rational. But it was obvious that he was not among rational or calm people. Ramsey was in a room full of wild blood thirsty hyenas. He had to be a lion to save Kinkay, and one thing lions don't do is talk. Ramsey pumped a round into Michael stomach. The dinner roll descended from Michael's hand as his natural reflex caused him to reach for his wound. No one flinched, never allowing hers eyes to leave Ramsey's Heaven sipped her wine as Michael hit the floor.

"Looks like Kinkay won't be the only one bleeding out."

'Fuck' thought Michael. 'This fucker shot me.'

Easy Mikey it's a gut wound, but it's the liver, you'll die from the poison before you bleed out.

'I'm gonna die' thought Michael. Ramsey stepped forward, training his gun on Matt.

"Detective Ramsey is it," started Heaven "may I speak?"

"I'd be quick about it if I were you…that was a liver shot I threw out there" retorted Ramsey.

Mikey, listen to me. I know this is gonna sound crazy but you have to trust me. I need you to stop your heart. It's the only chance we've got to give Heaven enough time to get us to a Dr. and get us stitched up before there's too much poison.

'Do it Michael, he's right' said Heaven telepathically.

"I'm sure your main goal is save this beautiful woman," began Heaven. I propose this. You take this woman of yours and you run, run until your legs feel like dead weight. And after all that running detective, Run!"

The carving knife Marr threw came so quickly Ramsey had no time to react. The shot he let off missed Matt by inches as Ramsey dodged the knife. Blood spilled from Kinkay's throat as Matt quickly sliced her open. Heaven grabbed the table cloth and used it to toss the contents on the table into the air. Ramsey let off another a blind round, but it was too late, Matt, Marr, and Heaven had already made their escape.

Chapter 54

Ramsey let off two more rounds, almost clipping Matt as he rounded the corner. Kinkay was bleeding profusely. Ramsey quickly took off his shirt and wrapped it around Kinkay's throat, applying pressure to the wound. The slice didn't cut the jugular vein, Kinkay could survive from the wound if she didn't bleed out. Ramsey could hear the sirens blaring far off from the east.

"Hold on Kinkay. Help is coming. Fuck."

Michael had finally stopped his heart. It was hard to concentrate with all the commotion, but he'd done it. The blood flow to the wound had been cut in half. Michael had never been dead before. For some reason he felt at peace.

Ramsey had to check on Officer Sloan, reluctantly he left Kinkay's side. Ramsey watched as Sloan's breaths grew shorter and shorter. Ramsey proudly inhaled death as it consumed Sloan and his chest slowly stopped rising and falling.

Suddenly Michael's peaceful experience with death turned into a choice. Michael could not deduce or even begin to understand what was going on, but it was like a dream. A dream where you have no idea what is going on but you instinctively know what you have to do to a certain extent. And Michael's extent was this choice. There were no doors or people standing in front of him. Everything was dark, but something was making him feel like he had a choice to make, go left, or go right.

Ramsey rose to walk away from Michael, and then out of nowhere a migraine unknown to man collapsed Ramsey to his knees on the spot. The pain caused his eyes to roll into the back of his head. His breaths became short and quick, his heart raised sporadically. Ramsey could do nothing; his mind had been shut off. His ability to analyze and counter had been compromised.

The choice to go left was not a hard one for Michael. Heaven's voice had echoed to him somehow, and it was coming from the left. The last thing Michael remembered was Heaven telling him telepathically that she would come for him, right before his last heartbeat.

The ordeal with Ramsey had lasted all but sixty seconds. Ramsey staggered to his feet, slowly regaining his balance. 'What the fuck was that' thought Ramsey. Out of nowhere the smell of gas filled Ramsey's nostrils. The smell was very feint but for some reason it was crashing Ramsey's nose. The sirens where much closer now, but for whatever reason Ramsey could hear more than just the sirens.

"Kinkay!" Ramsey rushed to her side. There was no time to waste, the house could be rigged to blow at any second. Ramsey picked up Kinkay with greater ease then he thought he could and started to make his way back to the service entrance.

THERE' S NO TIME, HEAD UPSTAIRS TO THE BATHROOM.

Ramsey bolted for the window with Kinkay cradled in his arms. He managed to steal a chance to glance back at Officer Sloan only to discover that Sloan was gone.

Chapter 55

Ramsey's first instinct was to jump out the window with Kinkay in his arms. He remembered the layout of the home like it was imprinted in his memory. He not only remembered the layout, he remembered details that he couldn't recall noticing in the first place. Such as, the thickness of the bush, the exact distance between the ground and the window, along with the distance from the window to the bush

THE DEVIL IS IN THE DETAIL.

Ramsey whirled around like a tornado to confront whoever was talking to him only to discover no one was there.

'What the fuck.'

WE HAVE NO TIME FOR THIS. WE HAVE TO KILL MICHAEL AND THE REST OF THIS NEST. QUICKLY, WE MUST RETRIEVE THE KNIFE.

Ramsey thought he was losing his mind, he was hearing a voice but not voices like most people who were just bat shit crazy. He was hearing a distinct voice that was giving clear and direct instructions. The sirens were growing excruciatingly louder, Kinkay's blood loss was breaching critical and the smell of gas had become nauseating for Ramsey. And now he was hearing a voice. This was too much for Ramsey. Ramsey picked up Kinkay and prepped himself to jump out the window. As Ramsey readied himself to sprint towards the window with Kinkay cradled in his arms something felt like it stabbed him in the gut. Once again his nose was filled with an aroma. But this smell wasn't strong or overbearing. It was sweet and comforting as if it were calling him. The initial pain had dropped Ramsey to one knee.

ITS THE KNIFE. IT WONT LET US LEAVE WITHOUT IT. WE ARE ALL CONNECTED. LEAVE THE GIRL. SHE' LL ONLY SLOW US DOWN. BESIDES, SHES BEEN SCENTED. THEYLL NEVER STOP CHASING HER.

Ramsey stood to his feet, still holding Kinkay in his arms. Ramsey broke out in full stride at top power and speed towards the window. Right before he was about to jump an unquenchable surge of fire raged through his body causing him to almost go into shock. Ramsey collapsed to his knees, dropping Kinkay hard to the floor. Ramsey struggled to control his labored breathing, supporting himself with one hand as he knelt. Kinkay had bled so much Ramey's black t-shirt had turned a grim dark burgundy color.

WE MUST RETRIEVE THE KNIFE.

"I don't know what the fuck you're talking about" yelled Ramsey.

JUST LET IT GUIDE YOU.

Ramsey rose to his feet then lifted Kinkay into his arms and slowly started making his way towards the same hall Heaven and everyone else escaped down. Kinkay wasn't moving. Ramsey had managed to check her for a feint pulse.

LEAVE HER. SHE WILL ONLY GET IN THE WAY.

"Shut the fuck up, or so help me God I'll just take a seat right here you fuckin, you fuckin, whateva the fuck you are."

Ramsey was angry, not because he was in a house filling with gas, and a person he cared deeply about was dying in his arms. Ramsey was upset because he didn't know what was going on. He didn't have control of the situation and it was making it hard for him to think.

Whatever it was that was pulling Ramsey was doing a spectacular job. It was as if Ramsey was a moth in search of flame that burned so strong that its very heat had become some sort of homing beacon that Ramsey was hard wired into. Ramsey was being drawn upstairs, which is definitely where he didn't want to go in a house filling up with natural gas. Ramsey couldn't help but notice the extravagant paintings, and the palace like layout of the hallway. Even while rushing it was hard not to notice. But while rushing Ramsey couldn't shake this feeling, like he'd been here before.

Once at the top of the stairs Ramsey was drawn to Heaven's room. Ramsey knew this was not the best place to be right now but the magnetism to this knife was uncontrollable. Ramsey opened the doors and headed straight for Heaven's bathroom. Ramsey was surprised he didn't take a second to take in his surroundings, his level of familiarity of a room he'd never been in before left an eerie feeling inside him.

Ramsey opened the door of the bathroom and there it was, laying on the bathroom floor, the knife. With no light it still sparkled, as if it created its own sun to show off its twinkle. Ramsey slowly walked into the bathroom. He could still hear the sirens, but for some reason the knife was drowning them out. He could hear car doors opening and slamming, tires screeching, and commands being distributed. Ramsey also took note of the gas; it was time to get out of here. Ramsey knelt down to pick up the knife, not wanting to bother with putting Kinkay down and then picking her back up, but when he touched the knife Ramsey had no choice but to drop Kinkay. The inscriptions and hieroglyphics instantaneously started emitting rays of light. Memories not of his own shot through Ramsey as if they were being uploaded like a flash drive. The experience had only taken seconds but it felt like Ramsey was watching a movie with no end in sight.

YOU ARE HIM.

It only took one explosion to jar Ramsey back into the present. The gas had been ignited and the house was going fast. The second explosion rocked the floor boards as the fire continued to mix with the gas. Ramsey hurriedly picked up Kinkay and made his way out the bathroom. Flames were converging on Ramsey from both sides. It was as if the fire was two deranged blood hounds with only Ramsey's scent on their mind.

Ramsey quickly turned back into the bathroom. With no time to think Ramsey took two long strides and leapt into the tub. The fire was on Ramsey's heals as he landed into the tub. The flames worked almost like claws as they tore away at Ramsey's clothes and back.

Suddenly out of nowhere the cast iron tub was propelled into the air. Ramsey did his best to shield to Kinkay as debris from the explosion landed on top of them. And then just as quickly as it sounded like World War III had broken out, there was complete silence. Ramsey was surprisingly still conscience. His brain was registering every bone that ached within his body.

JUST BREATHE MY BOY. YOUR WOUNDS WILL HEAL FASTER THAN YOU EXPECT.

The Epilogue

Chapter 1

YOU HAVE TO BE STRONGER, QUICKER, AND SMARTER THAN THEM AND YOU HAVE TO PUSH YOURSELF.

Ramsey could feel his bones aching, as he continued to move. The five-pound ankle and wrist weights made the task at hand almost unbearable. The past year had been crazy for Ramsey. He'd spent the first half of the year on the run with Kinkay. The Voices made it impossible for Ramsey to buy her enough time to recover properly. For their sake Ramsey managed to learn how to mask his scent.

CONCENTRATE BY TURNING OFF YOUR CONVENTIONAL WAYS OF USING YOUR SENSES.

Ramsey stopped moving. He'd been tracking this Voice in the jungle for hours. It was the final stage of his training. Ramsey had killed Voices before, but he never hunted them. Just stalking and subduing the man, with the Voice, was hard enough. After giving his prey a one-hour head start, Ramsey was now in the middle of the forest, tracking him. Ramsey cleared his head.

THATS IT.

The heightened sounds of the birds died out. Rain splashed the ground around him, the rain that once sounded like grenades turned into bridges of sound that echoed a path, straight to his prey. Nature had become Ramsey's ally. Ramsey instinctively switched gears. He moved with the wind, instead of against it. He could feel his prey's heart beat rising. The prey knew Ramsey was getting closer. Ramsey came to a small river bank that careened around the forest. Without thought, he stopped. Everything around him turned to a pale dark. Sound became his eyes. Ramsey stood at the bank of the river. Slowly, he put his back to the river, as he attempted to hone in on his prey.

The prey attacked quickly, rising out of the water just high enough to snatch Ramsey by his ankles and pull him into the river. The power of the current announced itself immediately. Ramsey was going under fast

LEAVE THEM ON.

Forced to abandon his first instinct of slipping off the weights, Ramsey quickly went for his knife. Ramsey wasn't strong enough to get out of the river, with the weights still on him, but he knew a fight to the death under water did not tip the scales in his favor at all. So, Ramsey allowed the weights to take him to the bottom of the eight-foot-deep river. Ramsey's feet barely touched the bottom before the man attacked again. Ramsey attempted to block the blow, but the water made him way too slow. The blow hit Ramsey, square in the chest, knocking him to the bed of the river. What surprised Ramsey more than the pain of the blow, was the power and speed by which it was administered. It was as if there was no current fighting against the man.

FOCUS.

Just as the man rushed Ramsey, with what seemed would to be his final kill move everything slowed down. Surprisingly, the man wasn't moving as fast anymore to Ramsey. The water magically showed pockets of space and air, and the currents that harassed the bed of the river, now moved in a pattern that made sense to Ramsey.

The golden handle of the dagger gleamed, as it rested on the rivers mattress. With the current flowing in his favor, Ramsey made his move. Fortunately, Ramsey's prey reacted to Ramsey's motion for the knife which then gave Ramsey the split second advantage he needed. Instead of going for the knife, his prey underestimated him and lunged for Ramsey. Using the current to increase his speed, Ramsey slid into the knife like a stolen base. The current gave Ramsey the speed he needed to reach the knife before his prey realized the tables had been turned. The piercing was quick and unexpected for Ramsey. His instincts were running on an entirely different level. Ramsey used the bed of the river, along with its current, to deliver an uppercut, with the knife, right through his prey's face.

Ramsey dragged his feet as he slowly made his way back to the cabin. His body was sore all over. All he could think about was Kinkay rubbing him down with her soft hands. Ramsey and Kinkay had become inseparable within the past year. Ramsey thought it would never happen again, but he was actually falling in love. Ramsey's sweet thoughts of Kinkay were interrupted, by a high pitched whistle. It wasn't just a whistle though; it was a tune.

"Is that the theme to Kill Bill?' questioned Ramsey.

I BELIEVE SO MY YOUNG WARRIOR.

Ramsey removed his weights and drew his knife.

"NOT A BAD IDEA. "

Suddenly, the whistling was coming from two different directions, northeast and northwest.

"Kinkay," screamed Ramsey.

RUN.

Ramsey ran faster than even his new companion thought was possible. Without thinking, Ramsey ran blindly into the small tucked away cabin that he and Kinkay had been sharing, for the past two months.

The place was ransacked. Everything was turned upside down, everything except the kitchen table. On the table rested a note. Ramsey's dread of the note's contents made walking to the table nearly impossible. Finally, Ramsey reached the note only to read the words.

VA rue veto serrqbz oheaf oevtug juvyr vaqrcraqrapr erfg frpher va ure yrsg.

12:00 est. 07/02 .... Tick Tock.

End

35650033R10148

Made in the USA
Middletown, DE
11 October 2016